Pure Bred

The Shelter Series, Book Four

Kate Sherwood

About The Book You have Purchased

Pure Bred

Seb Tanner takes a summer job with a community organization in a disadvantaged Seattle neighborhood because he wants to network, have some fun, and, sure, help out. It'll be like the Peace Corps without the annoyance of having to get extra vaccinations.

But the neighborhood he's working in is Trey Fiso's stomping grounds, and Trey doesn't appreciate spoiled rich boys coming in and trying to tell the locals how to run their lives.

When things get rough, the neighborhood expects Seb to run back to his safe life, but he surprises everyone, including himself. He turns his condo into a sanctuary for Trey as he recovers from a beating, and the two discover they have more in common than they thought.

Still, their worlds are too different, and Seb comes from the kind of people Trey's spent his life fighting *against*. When the two discover just how close Seb is to literally being the enemy, they know they have to be smart and stay away from each other. Of course, Trey's never been known for being smart, and Seb's learning a lot from Trey this summer...

Word Count: 67,207

Genre: Gay Contemporary Romance

Warning: This book contains graphic language and sexually explicit content. Intended for adult audiences only. Not intended for anyone under the age of 18.

Chapter One

TRISTAN'S LIVING ROOM WAS CROWDED. Seemed like it was always crowded these days, even more than it used to be, and Trey didn't like it. Seemed like everything was changing way too fast and he was getting left behind. He'd never been quick, but that didn't use to matter, not when he was just hanging out with everyone at Tristan's.

Now, though? There was a guy *in a suit* standing by the window where Trey usually stationed himself. The guy had taken off his jacket and loosened his tie when he'd seen how everyone else was dressed, but as far as Trey was concerned the damage had been done. Once a suit, always a suit. And Trey didn't trust suits.

He also didn't trust assholes who took his spot by the window. So he lurked in the kitchen, glaring at the interloper and scowling at the rest of the crowd, who all seemed totally fascinated by this visitor.

"So I don't think we'll find success with court challenges," the suit was saying. "We're certainly willing to help support you with any legal actions that make sense, but our organization is running on a limited budget; we can't afford to throw money or time away on long shots. The strategy we'd like to follow in this situation is based more on lobbying and publicity. The two fires give us a strong human-interest angle. They might have been designed to intimidate, but as long as we don't let that happen, I think we can make them work in our favor."

Trey cut his gaze over toward Jake. The guy's brother had *died* in one of the fires the suit was talking about, so it probably didn't sound good to hear them being treated as a positive. But Jake looked stoic enough. Micah was holding his hand pretty tight, though. Micah might be a junkie, but he wasn't stupid.

"So, moving forward," the suit said, "We'll want to be working with some of you quite closely in order to fine tune our message and make sure we're presenting it in the most positive way." He glanced around the room, and Trey didn't think he was imagining it when the suit's eyes seemed to rest on him for a little longer than the others. "Some of you will likely be most effective in the background," he said, and Trey snorted softly. Yeah. The background, that was where he belonged.

"But everyone's contributions will be important," the suit continued. "And in order to help coordinate it all and to ensure that communication is as streamlined as possible, we're going to assign a dedicated staff member—well, an intern—to this project for the next four months. I'd like to introduce you all to Seb Tanner." He raised an arm as if he was going to offer a hug, then gripped the new guy's shoulder instead.

Seb Tanner was a suit. He wasn't *wearing* a suit, but that didn't change what he was. His khakis were pressed, his light blue button-down starched and properly tucked in, his blond hair flipped in a tidy wave across his tanned forehead. Suit-on-vacation, suit-casual, junior-suit—the precise definition didn't matter, because they all featured the word *suit*. Even his smile was suit-worthy, confident and friendly, as if this guy had never in his life been introduced to someone who wasn't absolutely thrilled to meet him and really, really hoped to be able to get to know him better.

"Thanks, Gary," Tanner said, and smiled at the older man as if Tanner was the one in charge and the main suit had just been allowed to make an introduction. Then he turned to the room. "I want you all to know that I've been reading the file on this for two days straight, and I'm appalled by what I've seen. Gentrification is one thing, but the high-pressure tactics, the intimidation, the disregard for human life or property?" Tanner shook his head. "It's the kind of situation that made me want to get involved in community organizing and public interest work in the first place. I'm proud to be a part of this movement, and I'm looking forward to fighting on your behalf."

"For four months." It was Simon, his eyebrow raised as he looked Tanner over. Yeah, if there was anyone in the crowd who'd be able to out-confident someone like Suit, Jr., it would be Simon.

"You're passionate about the project, you're going to fight, fight, fight... for four months. And then you'll go back to school, I assume? But this 'project' isn't going to be finished in four months. Is it?"

Tanner kept his gaze locked on Simon's but didn't even look flustered. "I'm here to do what I can within the time frame I have available. I'm hoping to work with locals to set up communications and establish a general structure to use going forward. But, no, I wouldn't expect the project to be finished by the end of the summer. That's why Gary is here, to ensure continuity."

Simon sat back, but didn't look completely satisfied. Trey shifted impatiently. Contacting the Seattle Communities Team had been Simon's brilliant idea, so if he wasn't happy with the way things were going, it wasn't likely that anyone else in the room was any more satisfied. But this meeting was Simon's baby; if he wasn't going to fight, no one else would, either.

But that didn't mean they wouldn't cast meaningful glances at each other. And it looked like Suit, Jr., was picking up on those looks, and the unrest behind them. "I know you guys started this," he said softly. "I know you've done a lot to get the resistance off the ground. And I know I'm young, and not an expert. But I have access to experts, and I have time. This is my only job, my only priority, for the next four months. I think we can all work together, and I think we can make things happen. I wouldn't be here if I thought I couldn't be useful."

He sounded like he actually believed it. Like he'd lived a life where being useful and wanted was the default position for him and he saw no reason why that situation should change.

What a shithead.

~*~*~*~

SEB WASN'T USED TO FACING this kind of skepticism. He wasn't used to people looking at him as if he was an outsider who had to *earn* their respect instead of just receiving it because of who he was. Who his family was.

He loved it.

He'd rise to the challenge, he'd show them he was worthwhile, he'd have them eating out of his hand within—well, okay, he shouldn't get carried away. There'd be no hand-feeding, although there were a couple of them whose mouths he wouldn't mind getting to know a little better. But, no, that wasn't what he was there for. If he wanted something like that, if he wanted to find a rough, tough guy to put him in his place—and looking out at this crowd, he was pretty sure that was *exactly* what he wanted—he'd find it somewhere else. Don't mix business with pleasure. *And damn it, Seb, keep your mind on your job!*

He checked that his face was still wearing its expression of interest and admiration for Gary, then let himself scan the audience again. It was a strange crowd, a mix of almost-grown-up street kids with a couple guys nearly as preppy as himself, then some older people—social workers, small business owners, community members—that sort of thing. About twenty people who had apparently become the core of the resistance to the area's anti-gentrification push. And a cat, lolling on the back of a sofa like she was the queen inspecting her subjects, and a little dog who clearly thought he was the host *and* bouncer for the occasion. Quite a mix.

Seb's eye was caught by the guy standing in the little kitchenette. Damn. A perfect mix of physical power and emotional frustration. If Seb was lucky, maybe throw in a little self-loathing homophobia and get a fuck to remember. Oh, yeah. The guy was built like an oversized gymnast—fairly tall, but still somehow giving the impression of compact strength. He'd be totally impersonal, totally in control. No kissing or any of that shit, unless—oh, god, yeah, unless he bent Seb over and *bit him*, like a lion controlling his mate.

Seb felt his cock shift and pulled his mind back to what he was supposed to be thinking about. Yeah, yeah, plans for the next meeting, smaller sub-groups working on different goals, all the stuff he and Gary had talked about on the drive over. The importance of working as a team. Sweaty, angry sex was an effective team-building tool, wasn't it? Yeah, he should consider that as a possible topic for his senior thesis. He'd done a term in England the year before and gotten a good start on his research— he could go for a little cross-cultural flair and title it *Non-traditional power exchanges in modern business relationships—*

economically valid reasons to 'fancy a bit of rough'. Hell, yeah. He could get that published.

"Right, Sebastian?" Gary said, and Seb smiled enthusiastically, if somewhat vaguely. Gary didn't seem like the type to go off script, so, sure, he was probably right.

The meeting wrapped up then and Gary guided Seb out as soon as they could manage without seeming rude. "They need a little time to think it all through, and we'll support them as they do that. But this is an emotional situation for them, and we're pushing them to think strategically, not emotionally."

"They did *ask* for help," Seb said as they walked down the street to Gary's car. "Do we really have to persuade them to take something when they were the ones who asked for it in the first place?" And then, totally unbidden, the image of the ripped guy from the kitchenette making Seb ask for it, making him beg—holy shit, he needed to get laid. This was getting stupid.

"People often have a general idea of what they're looking for," Gary explained, apparently oblivious to Seb's distraction. "But when we arrive and start making things concrete, they may not be as pleased. Often they just want us to give them money, but our funding doesn't allow for that. We offer expertise, not cash."

Seb nodded. The kitchenette guy had seemed resentful, and this context made his reaction make sense. It also made it a bit more difficult to be turned on by his anger. The guy was just as angry at *Gary* as he was at Seb, and there was absolutely nothing sexy about Gary, not unless you were kinky to an extreme Seb

7

didn't even want to begin contemplating. "So we give them some space and they realize they need us and come running back with their tails between their legs?"

"They aren't dogs, Sebastian. And we need them just as much as they need us—our mission statement involves working *with* communities to address social issues. If we can't carry out our mission, there isn't much reason for us to exist as an organization."

Seb didn't answer that. He didn't like the idea of needing anyone. Wanting? Oh, he was just fine with wanting. But need was a different thing altogether.

"And I don't think space is going to be the answer," Gary continued. "Not for this group. They've got some strong personalities at work, and they're already fairly well connected in terms of community leaders. They're primed and ready to go, and if we give them too much time, they're going to start acting on their own, without our advice and expertise. They'll either have initial success, in which case it will be difficult for us to persuade them we can offer any more help, or they'll have initial failure, which will mean we have a lot of cleaning up to do. I'd rather avoid both scenarios."

"So what's the plan?" Seb asked. Gary didn't have a lot of flair, didn't have that flash of brilliance that attracted Seb to people, but he knew what he was doing. And he was, technically, Seb's boss this summer, although Seb preferred to think of him as a guide or mentor.

"I want you in there with them. You're young; a lot of them are young. I want you to build on that, get to know them, earn their trust."

"It sounds like I'm going undercover." Seb wasn't objecting to the idea; actually, it sounded intriguing.

But stick-in-the-mud Gary shook his head. "Be honest. Get them to trust you by being worthy of their trust. We're on their side in all this."

"Yeah, okay," Seb agreed. He was already thinking back to the guy in the kitchen, the barely hidden anger, the muscles—he could spend some time with him, for sure. And, really, to know Seb was to love him. There shouldn't be any problem with the rest of his assignment. "I'm in," he said. "I'm ready."

Gary didn't look entirely convinced, but that was Gary's problem. Seb smiled to himself and let his mind wander. He'd made a good decision when he took this internship. It was going to be a very interesting summer.

Kate Sherwood

Chapter Two

"COULDN'T WE JUST GO BACK at them the same way they came at us?" Trey asked. The new people had left, thank Christ, and it was just the regular gang flopped over Tristan's ragged sofas, sorting through their impressions of the meeting. "Why are we dealing with suits and talking about lobbying and publicity and whatever the fuck else they're saying? These guys *attacked* us. They're trying to burn us out and we're going to *lobby them* to stop? No way. We need to hit back."

"Who do you plan to hit?" Simon asked. He sounded way too calm; the bastard *always* sounded way too calm. "Who are 'they', exactly?"

Okay, he had a point, but Trey wasn't ready to give up yet. "Okay, so *that's* what we need the suits for. They can figure that out, right? They figure out who's doing all this, and then we take care of them our way."

He looked around the room. Shane should be on his side; Shane always preferred to respond to things with his body, his fists, just like Trey did. Except Shane was all caught up in Noah these days, and Noah was—different. Noah had a future, a bright one, and Shane was turning himself inside out trying to be sure he didn't mess any of it up. Noah's dreams needed to come true, and Shane needed to keep himself clean enough that there'd be a place for him by Noah's side. That's how whipped Shane was.

So no matter what Shane's actual opinion was, he wouldn't be able to act on it.

Simon was too clean, too polished for anything rough, and Tristan? He wasn't clean, not by a long shot, but he wasn't a fighter. He had other ways of getting what he wanted, after all.

Becky and Amanda looked interested, but Trey didn't like that idea. They'd both be pissed if they knew he was leaving them out because they were chicks, but that was just too damn bad. He wasn't going to be part of any plan that might end up with either of them getting hurt.

So that left Micah and Jake. Micah was always ready to do anything stupid, and Jake? His damn brother had died in one of the fires—of course he'd be in. Not as many allies as Trey might have hoped for, but enough to be a start, at least.

"You find the target," he told Simon. Then he turned to look at Micah and Jake. "Then we'll pull the trigger."

"And who's the target?" Simon asked. "The thugs who actually did the work? Or the people who hired them?"

"Both," Jake said. Like Simon, his voice was quiet, and like Simon, he somehow drew attention anyway. He swallowed hard and had a bit more volume when he added, "I want them all. They've all got blood on their hands."

For a moment, Trey felt cheap. His tough-guy act, his hunger for mayhem without any real personal justification—in the face of Jake's true grief, his soul-deep need for revenge, Trey's impulses seemed petty. It wasn't a good feeling, so he pushed it down as quickly as he could and ignored it. He wanted things to be straightforward. He wanted the satisfaction of violence, the simplicity of anger. Nothing more complicated. No grief, no guilt. Just rage. "We'll find them," he told Jake. "All of them. And you're goddamn right—we'll make them pay."

Jake seemed satisfied with that and the meeting broke up without too much more discussion. Jake offered to drop Becky and Amanda off as he drove himself and Micah home, Noah and Shane headed for the door as well, and Trey—damn it.

Only a few months earlier, it wouldn't have been an issue. He'd just have slumped down on the couch, if Shane wasn't already sleeping on it, and Tristan would have gone on about his night without worrying about there being an extra person or two in his apartment.

But that had all changed when Simon moved in. Nobody'd said anything—Simon was way too smooth for that. But the silences that used to be casual had somehow gotten awkward, and now Tristan *didn't* just go on with his night, he sat there waiting, like Trey was someone who needed to be entertained, or at least watched. Like he was an unwelcome guest instead of a neutral piece of furniture. Tristan had a boyfriend, and the two of them wanted their privacy. Which meant Trey was out.

So he followed everyone else down to the street and pretended he had somewhere to go. Someone waiting for him.

And nobody asked him for any details. They just went on about their lives, and he started walking. He knew some spots, places to stay dry and warm for the night, and he'd be happy to have some peace and quiet, some time to himself without people yipping at him all the time. Yeah, this was good. It was a warm night; rich people paid a lot of money to buy tents and shit to go on camping trips, but he didn't need all that. It was practically summer and it wasn't raining; perfect night for sleeping under the stars.

That was all he needed. A spot at the park, worked into the undergrowth enough that the pigs wouldn't show up and hassle him, and he was fine. He was great.

He had absolutely nothing to complain about.

Except for the assholes who'd thought they had the right to come into his neighborhood and start throwing their weight around. *They* were the damn problem. Everything else was fine. But when he got his hands on the assholes starting the fires? They'd wish they'd never learned how to light a damn match.

BEER. IT SHOULD HAVE MADE Seb happy. Not in a frat-boy drink-til-you-puke way; he was too old for that high school bullshit. No, this was more sophisticated, a deep, dark ale with a distinctive roasted malt taste that balanced perfectly with the English hops. That's what the menu said, anyway. Seb schooled his expression and took a big gulp, refused to allow his nose to wrinkle at the bitterness, and smiled. "Nice," he said. And then another gulp, because he needed to finish the glass and might as well get it over with all at once. Maybe his taste buds would go numb, if he was lucky.

"It's my new go-to brew," Brock said, as proud as if he'd created the beer himself.

Allison sipped appreciatively. "It's got real substance, but it doesn't feel heavy." She kept the ostentatiously oversized wine glass in her hand as she leaned into the leather bench. "We should get some for the house," she told Talbot.

Drinking beer, and then talking about beer. Very hipster, and totally typical. Brock was Seb's cousin and oldest friend; Allison was Seb's sister, Talbot her husband. Seb was closer to them than to anyone else in the world, and they were boring him to death. If he substituted a few phrases, he could imagine his parents having the exact same conversation at a wine tasting with *their* friends.

"I'm thinking about becoming an anti-capitalist radical," he announced at the next slight break in the conversation.

Allison nodded. "Is that your obsession for this week?"

"You think they want you?" Talbot asked, his smile gentle but maybe a little patronizing. "I'm not sure they're doing a lot of recruiting from the one-percent these days."

Brock didn't even answer, just leaned back and made eye contact with their pretty brunette server, gesturing that the table needed another round.

It was exactly how Seb would have reacted if one of them had come out with a similar statement, but recognizing that made the situation more annoying, not less. "There is some pretty awful stuff going on, right here in Seattle." He dredged his memory for details. "Arson, murder, all over a few blocks of real estate. It's pretty serious."

"This is from your internship?" Allison asked. "They've got you working on a case where someone got *murdered*?"

"Yeah." Damn, he wished he'd payed a bit more attention to it all. This was better than talking about beer, but he wasn't going to be able to keep it up for long if he couldn't supply more information. "Some guys deliberately burned a building down *with people inside it*. Three of them died."

"I read about that," Talbot said. "It was in the paper." He looked at Allison, then back at Seb. "It's really serious, isn't it? I mean, people are *dying*. Is this something you should be getting yourself involved in?"

"We just want you to be safe," Allison said.

Of course they did. Seb was the baby of the family, not only the youngest sibling but the youngest of all the cousins as well. He took advantage of the situation when it pleased him, allowing himself to be spoiled and coddled. But now?

"It's not that dangerous, and it's actually interesting. I'm actually *doing* something, you know? I'm being useful."

"But careful, too," Allison prompted. "If you're not comfortable with something—"

"It's okay to say 'no', sweetie," Brock said, his voice a fairly eerie imitation of Seb's mother. "You don't need to let anyone push you into doing anything you're not ready for."

"I think that was more her speech to me than to Seb," Allison said.

And the conversation somehow segued into shared memories of parental advice and dubious wisdom. Stories they'd all lived through together, all remembered together, and would all continue to talk about for as long as they had breath.

It was all so—comfortable.

That was all. There was no big trauma here, nothing for anybody to get upset about.

The only thing that wasn't business-as-usual was Sebastian's restless, inner snarling in reaction to it all. What the hell was wrong with him?

He let the conversation flow on without him and tried to sort himself out. He wasn't a moody person, not typically.

Shit. It was that guy from the meeting. Well, not that guy, specifically, but Seb's *reaction* to that guy. He'd had sex recently, sure—Grindr worked pretty damn well in an urban center like

Seattle. But it had just been sex. There hadn't been the edge, the thrill of apprehension that bordered on fear, the excitement of being right next to something—someone—who might not follow all the rules polite society demanded.

Yeah. Seb didn't need to get fucked, he needed to take the chance of getting fucked *up*. He drained his glass, barely noticing the bitterness, and shifted around to find his wallet. "I'm going to head out. Big day tomorrow—got to help lots of junkies steal buildings from hard-working citizens. Need my beauty sleep."

Brock raised a sardonic eyebrow but didn't say anything; he could know Seb was full of shit without having to *announce* that he knew. Allison smiled blandly and presented her cheek for a kiss, while Talbot scoffed at Seb's attempt to pull out his wallet and cover his share of the tab.

They were his family, and he loved them. But there was something crawling under his skin, something scratching at him from the inside out, and he needed to get away from them all. And once he made it safely outside he needed to figure out what to do to calm himself down. *Who* to do. And where to find him…

Chapter Three

"I'M NOT FUCKING *READING* all that. This isn't school, and you sure as hell aren't my teacher. No way." It was the day after the big meeting and Trey was back at Tristan's apartment, but it wasn't a relaxing sanctuary anymore, not with the junior suit sitting across the kitchen table from him. Trey wanted to storm out of the apartment, but the shithead might take that as a retreat, and there was no way Trey would let anyone think he was running away. He didn't run away from anything.

Junior Suit sighed like he was disappointed, but not exactly surprised. "So how do you see yourself contributing to the movement?" he asked. "We're essentially being detectives at this stage—looking for similar resistances that have been successful, trying to find any weaknesses in our opponents. Trying to figure out who our opponents even *are* would be a good start. If you don't want to read…?" Junior raised his eyebrows questioningly, and for the first time Trey noticed the shadow on his cheek. More than just a shadow.

"What happened to your face?" Trey demanded. It was none of his business, of course, but better to talk about that than about the stupid papers in front of him. "That bruise—it wasn't there yesterday."

Junior's hand lifted half-way to his face before he caught himself and lowered it. "Slips, trips, and falls," he said. "The most common types of workplace injury."

It wasn't a real answer, obviously, but then Tristan and Simon finished up the breakfast dishes and sat down with them and Trey let the bruise drop out of the conversation. He let *himself* drop out of the conversation, really, and just sat there as the others debated strategies and schedules and whatever.

It wasn't like he didn't want to help. He just—he wasn't great at reading, and he wasn't great at sitting still, and he wasn't great at thinking about things or being a fucking detective, and he definitely wasn't great at being patient and calm when some stranger was trying to make him do a bunch of shit he wasn't great at.

He pushed to his feet, somehow knocking his chair over in the process, and the other three turned to stare at him. "I'll *do* things," he said, leaving the chair where it lay. "If you need stuff done, tell me. But all this?" He frowned down at the already confusing mass of papers and laptops on the kitchen table. "This isn't for me. You guys figure it all out, and then I'll take care of what needs to be done."

"We're not looking for vigilantism," Junior Suit said. He sounded—what, amused?

"I don't give a shit what you're looking for. This isn't about *you*, it's about us." He ignored the suit then and turned his gaze to Simon. "All of us, not just you and what you think is best. You've got connections and a good brain—that's fine. We can use both of those things. But you're new to all this, and you don't get to take over just because you're smart or because you're fucking Tristan. That's not how it's going to go."

"I'm not trying to take over," Simon said. Calm, like always. Making Trey feel like a little kid having a tantrum. Like always.

"I need to move the furniture back," Tristan said. It sounded like it was coming out of the blue, but it probably wasn't. Tristan was usually pretty good at following what was going on. "It's still shoved around from the meeting yesterday. Trey, give me a hand?"

Trey wanted to object, but given that he'd just *said* he'd do what needed to be done, there was no real way to say no. So he started by lifting up his own chair and replacing it at the table, then followed Tristan the few steps into the living room area of the small apartment.

"Get that end," Tristan said.

It was a relief to do something simple, and Trey bent to find a good grip before lifting gently. It was a sofa-bed with a heavy old-style frame to it, so Tristan had to work pretty hard to carry his share of the weight. That was satisfying, at least; Trey was good for *something*.

They moved the rest of the furniture back to where it belonged, then stood by the window as Tristan massaged his palms like they were sore. He was kind of exaggerating, obviously, and from someone else Trey would have resented it. But Tristan was Tristan. He meant well.

"It could get ugly," Tristan finally said. He was looking out toward the street. "People have already died."

"Yeah. They've already died; it's already ugly."

Tristan's nod was slow, but seemed genuine. "Okay. Right. That's a better way to think of it, I guess. It's already ugly. But right now it's on the DL, at least. You know? They're making sneak attacks, but it's not a flat-out war."

"Maybe it should be."

"Maybe. But maybe not. Because if we start a war? I don't know how we win. And I don't want to be responsible for the people who get hurt. Do you?"

Of course Trey didn't want *other* people to get hurt. He wasn't worried about himself, but anyone else? No, he wanted them to be safe. "So what are you saying? What should we do?"

"Sit tight." Tristan smiled ruefully. "I know, waiting isn't your thing, but for now? If you start something... well, you'd have no idea who to start it *with*, not yet. And once we do know, if you start something we can't be sure they'll come back after *you*. You know? It could be any of us. Could be Becky or Amanda, could be Mr. or Mrs. Nguyen at the store, could be anyone."

Chicks and old people. Shit. Tristan knew him way too well. "So I do nothing?"

Tristan shrugged. "It's up to you, obviously, but I was thinking it might be good to start setting up—I don't know what to call it. When Simon does it he's networking, connecting all the business owners and parents and retired people—"

"All the people who look at me like I'm about to beat them up or rob their stores," Trey prompted. He knew exactly the sort of people Simon was networking with.

"They're members of the community. But, yeah, I think Simon's a better person to be in contact with them." Tristan sounded so smooth, but he was smirking and it made Trey feel like they were both on the same side again. It wasn't like any of the more respectable folks in the neighborhood would be too thrilled to deal with a former whore, either. Simon's past was no cleaner than anyone else's, but he was better at covering it up. "There are other people we need to be in touch with," Tristan continued. "Shane and Noah have already been working with lots of them, but they've focused on people with pets. I'm hoping we can expand that and reach out to everyone. Becky said she wanted to work on that, and she'd be great for connecting with people who might be kind of freaked out if you or Shane showed up—"

"There's no way you're sending Becks out there on her own. Not to the rougher places."

Tristan held up his hands. "I know. But if you went with her and just hung back a little, that'd be okay, right? She could talk to people without intimidating them, but you'd be around in case things went wrong."

A bodyguard. It actually sounded kind of perfect. Not much thinking, getting to protect someone, and the potential for some nice violence. "Maybe," Trey said. "But what's Becky going to actually be telling people?"

The answer came from the kitchen table, where Simon and the suit had apparently been eavesdropping. "We're setting up a communication network," Junior said. "We'll have social media accounts set up and people can contribute ideas, get information—"

"Social media?" Trey stared at him. "How the fuck are these people going to use social media? You think they've got their laptops with them? You think there's wi-fi in the fucking Jungle?"

And there it was, for the first time: Junior Suit seemed startled, unsure of himself. It was a good look on him.

"They don't even have phones?" he asked.

"Some might," Trey said. *He* did, although he didn't always have minutes to use and sure as hell didn't have a data plan. "But most of them?" He glanced over at Tristan for confirmation. "If you're wanting us to go after the people who are really fucked up? The junkies and the crazies and the rest? Nah. You can't count on them having phones."

Junior Suit looked at Simon, then Tristan, then finally back to Trey. "So how *can* we set up communications with them?" he asked.

Neither Tristan nor Simon answered; they just looked at Trey and waited.

And, sure, yeah, of the people in the room, he was the one closest to the people they were talking about. He didn't have Tristan's whoring money or Simon's education, and he sure as hell didn't have whatever Junior Suit was working with. So on this he actually had a bit of expertise to contribute.

"Face-to-face is best," he said. "There's bulletin boards, and the free newspapers, and we could hand out flyers, but a lot of them don't read too well. Even if they know how they might not bother. But most of them will talk to people, if they trust you." He looked at the other three. "If they trust *me*," he corrected, 'cause there was no way the others had a prayer. "Or Becks. Yeah, she'll be good at this. But… I don't mean to sound like an asshole, but why are we bothering? I mean, what ideas do you think they're going to be contributing? Why do you want to give them information? They're not…" He tried to find the right words. "They're not much use. They can't even take care of themselves, you know? I mean, I'm sure there's some really sweet-smelling bullshit we could spread around, but seriously: if they were on top of things, they wouldn't be living where they're living. *How* they're living."

How I'm *living*. But he didn't say that part out loud.

"Some of them have just fallen on hard times, maybe?" Suit seemed like he was asking a genuine question. "They're in temporary difficulties, but that doesn't mean—'not much use' is a pretty harsh description, surely?"

"They've got their own shit going on," Trey said. "Like, their own worries. If they *do* have any fucking 'ideas', they should be using them to figure out a way to get somewhere to live, not worrying about who owns a bunch of buildings they can't afford anyway."

"If gentrification of the neighborhood continues, they'll be pushed even further out," Suit said. "We've already seen pressure being applied to the ju—the addicts. Other people who don't fit into an upwardly mobile neighborhood will get the same treatment. It's in these people's self-interest to join our cause and help us resist."

"It's in these people's self-interest to figure out what they're going to eat today and where they're going to sleep. They don't have a whole lot of energy left over for long-term planning."

"Then we need to help them." Suit said it like it was obvious. Like it was possible.

"Yeah, I'll get right on that," Trey said.

"We aren't looking for miracles," Simon interjected. "We aren't expecting them to be master strategists or help us with research." Weren't expecting them to do any of the things Trey was refusing to do. "But we *are* hoping they'll trust us enough to be our eyes and ears. If we let them know what we're looking for and if we can figure out a way for them to get that information to us, they could be invaluable. And of course we need to ensure they're taking whatever precautions they can, now that we're dealing with outside violence coming to the neighborhood."

It was always hard to read Simon, but he seemed sincere. And Tristan loved him, so Trey gave him the benefit of the doubt. "We can warn them. Becks and me, and Shane and Noah. Getting them to be our spies? Yeah, I guess they might be able to do some of that. If we get the owners of the twenty-four hour stores on side, we could use them. If someone saw something important they could tell whoever's behind the counter at the corner store or the pharmacy or wherever, right? And that person could phone—I don't know, here?"

Tristan nodded. "It's not like I have to get up for work in the morning. Makes sense for me to field the calls."

It wasn't like many of them had to get up for work in the morning or any other time of day, but Tristan was still the logical choice. The apartment wasn't as friendly as it had been pre-Simon, but it was still home base for most of them.

And as if to prove that, there was a knock on the door and then the sound of it opening, with a familiar voice singing out, "Hi! Everybody decent?"

A moment later Becky appeared from the hallway. "Reporting for duty, sir!" She snapped off a not-bad salute in Simon's direction, then took the few extra steps to stand next to Trey and wrap her arm around his waist. Becky was a toucher, at least when she was in a good mood. "We got a plan?"

"Kinda," Trey said.

But it was enough. Sure, there were details to be sorted out, but he had something to do. He'd keep Becky safe and she'd talk to people and it wouldn't do any damn good in the end, but at least it'd be something. At least he would be a little bit useful.

Chapter Four

THERE WAS TOO MUCH TESTOSTERONE in the apartment. Seb felt like it was gusting through the air, landing on him, soaking in through his pores—making him horny as hell.

The guy the night before had been a disaster. Rough sex was one thing—it was one *hell* of a thing—but there had to be some damn sex involved to make it worthwhile. Pushing Seb around and demanding a blow job had been a reasonable start, but it damn sure shouldn't have been all there was. When Seb had gotten between the guy and the door, suggesting that he shouldn't be leaving before Seb got taken care of, he'd gotten a smack in the face for his efforts. And a bruise that didn't trigger any of the happy memories similar marks had provided in the past.

And now, in the dingy apartment with the tough guy—Trey— stalking around and glowering at everyone? Damn. Seb tracked the girl's arm as it wrapped around Trey's waist, could practically feel the solid strength of his body as she leaned into him, let himself imagine, just for a moment, the way *he* could lean in, and how Trey would catch him, pull him closer or push him away or do

29

whatever the hell he wanted, *take* whatever he wanted, use Seb's body as his own—but not fucking walk out before Seb got off. No, in this fantasy Trey was forceful, even rough, but not a complete asshole.

"So do we have flyers or something?" the girl asked, and she was looking at Seb like she expected him to have an answer. Shit, right, he was supposed to be organizing all this.

"Not yet." He tried not to look at Trey. "But we could put something together pretty fast, and there's a good photocopier at the office. I could run off a bunch of copies."

"Okay, good. Let's do it." The girl was practically vibrating with energy, and Seb tried to remember her from the day before. He was pretty sure she'd been sitting on the couch staring at her hands for the whole meeting. "What do we need on the flyers? Phone numbers? Contact information? Do we know enough about what we're doing to put any of that on?"

She let go of Trey and bounced across the floor toward Seb. He resisted the urge to step backward. "What have we got?" she demanded. Not mean, not even aggressive, but unsettlingly enthusiastic.

"Becks." It was Trey's voice, a low rumble that somehow managed to sound gentle at the very same time it sent an electric current through Seb's whole body. And then, after the one syllable, Trey said no more.

But Becky turned around anyway and looked at him, and there was clearly some sort of communication between them.

"I just..." She shook her head, then her whole body, like a dog after a bath. "Right," she said. "Okay. I'm going to—you know."

She lurched toward the door and Trey started after her, but stopped when Tristan raised a hand in his direction.

"Let me go," Tristan said. "If it's you, she'll just..."

There was a moment of clearly intense non-verbal arguing before Trey gave a dissatisfied huff, and shifted his weight back onto his heels. Tristan nodded as if in thanks and then jogged toward the door.

Seb felt like he was stuck at another family's dinner table while they had a below-the-surface brawl. So much history, too much unspoken communication, and he was ignorant of it all.

Probably just as well. He clapped his hands together with forced enthusiasm and said, "Okay. Should we draft up something to put on the flyers? If we're thinking of using 24-hour stores as communication hubs we should talk to the owners first, right? Should I do that?"

And there was another damn look, this time between Trey and Simon, the only ones left. "I should do that," Simon said finally. "They're worried, and they don't know you."

"Don't trust you," Trey said, as if the clarification was necessary.

"Don't I need them to *start* trusting me? Wouldn't it make sense for me to start building relationships with them?"

"The kind of relationship that starts with you asking them for a favor?" Trey raised an eyebrow, then shifted his attention to Simon. "Can you do it today?"

Simon nodded.

Seb felt like a little kid, and even worse, *sounded* like a little kid when he said, "So what am I supposed to do?"

Trey's expression was far too smug when he said, "Research. Be a fucking detective. Figure out who the enemy is. That's the stage we're at, right?"

That plan had seemed a lot more attractive when Seb had seen himself as the lead detective, directing others in their menial tasks. But now Tristan was gone, Simon seemed about to leave, and Trey had made it crystal damn clear that he wouldn't be helping. So Seb was on his own. Where was the fun in that?

And seriously, who were these assholes to think that *he*, Sebastian Tanner, wouldn't be good at persuading some shopkeepers to help the cause?

"I'm actually very good with people," he said.

"Yeah, you're fucking irresistible." Trey snorted, then looked at Simon. "The sooner the better. Becky's going to need a project."

Simon nodded. "I'll go out now." He looked at Seb, then Trey. "You two can stay here. Trey, you're in charge."

"In charge of *what*?" Seb demanded. He honestly wasn't sure about the cause and effect in the situation—was he acting like a petulant child because they were treating him that way, or was it actually the other way around?

32

"In charge of the apartment and anyone in it," Simon replied evenly. "This is Tristan's home; I can't leave a stranger here alone."

"So why don't we go back to my original idea of running this out of the organization offices? There's as much space there as there is here, but it's not somebody's home."

"This movement is about protecting this neighborhood—it should be based here. If you guys come up with some money for us to rent office space, that'd be great, but otherwise, we'll have to keep taking advantage of Tristan's hospitality."

"Don't worry," Trey said. "I'll keep an eye on him. He won't walk off with anything valuable."

Another look between them, one Seb *hoped* was a warning from Simon telling Trey not to go too far, and then Simon grabbed his jacket and a clipboard and left.

As soon as the apartment door clicked shut, Trey turned to Seb. "So what actually happened to your face?"

"Took a guy home and he was the wrong kind of rough. Not the kind I was looking for." Seb wasn't sure if he'd told the truth because he'd hoped to shock Trey or hoped to introduce the topic of sex, but he didn't get satisfaction on either front.

Trey just nodded as if Seb's story was about what he'd expected and then flopped onto the sofa and picked up the remote for the TV.

Seb was clearly dismissed and expected to get to work, but he perched on the arm of the opposite sofa instead. "That girl— Becky. What's her story? What was all that about?"

"Becks? Her story? Yeah, that's a long, tragic tale of none-of-your-fucking-business."

Seb shook his head, ignoring the warning. "She was kinda manic, but she didn't seem that way yesterday. So, drugs, or mental illness, or...?"

"The guy who got too rough with you last night," Trey said thoughtfully. "You get off on that? You like getting beat up? That's why you're shoving your nose into something I just fucking *said* was none of your business?"

"Yeah, I get off on it. But, no, I'm pushing my nose into this because—" Because why? Did Seb actually have a reason, or was he just making an excuse? "Because it might be a problem for the movement if one of our recruiters is off her head because of a chemical imbalance *or* chemical consumption."

"I'll be with her. She'll be fine." Trey cocked his head and Seb could practically see the hit being formulated. "Would it be a problem for the movement if one of our so-called leaders has a weird kink that gets him into dangerous situations?"

"There's no connection between that and my work."

"Bullshit. I barely know you, you're at work, and you've already told me about it. Who else are you going to tell about it, and how's that going to make people think of us?"

34

Jesus, Seb wished he could go back to the simple days of Trey being a barely verbal caveman. "I shouldn't have told you. Obviously. I have no plans to tell anyone else."

"You had no plans to tell me, either, did you? So you not having plans doesn't seem to do you much good."

"Are you actually concerned about this or are you just pushing me back on the Becky thing?"

"Do you still *need* to be pushed back on the Becky thing?"

"No."

Trey pressed a button on the remote and the TV clicked to life. "Then we're done."

Done. Trey stared at the screen as if he were alone in the room, and Seb skulked back into the kitchen. That conversation had been—what the hell had it been? Aggressive. Confrontational.

Arousing. Seb had never been turned on by a dangerous *conversation* before, and it was troubling that it was happening now. He was supposed to be a professional, and as Trey had just pointed out, he was screwing that up. His 'weird kink'—as if there were normal kinks—could actually end up getting him in trouble. Not criminal, no, but if Gary—strait-laced, serious Gary—heard about this? Not about the kink itself, but that Seb had for some unknown reason told this stranger about it, while working, while representing the organization…

Shit. It would be a mess.

An even bigger mess if the news somehow got back to his family. They were so sunny and happy and so fucking kind.

They'd accepted their *gay* son without too much trouble. But their gay son who wanted—needed—to be pushed around and humiliated and scared? That was a whole different thing.

Seb had to get his head on straight. He needed to stop antagonizing Trey, needed to avoid him altogether if this was what happened when they talked. Seb needed to be smart about this.

Yeah. Smart.

He let himself take one more look toward the sofa. Trey had his feet up on the coffee table, tree-trunk legs relaxed and far enough apart that Seb would be able to ease right between them. What would happen if he did that, right then? If he walked over— no, fuck it, *crawled* over—and eased into Trey's space, reached for his fly—Trey's hands would catch his, and he'd growl *Wait until you're told*, and Seb would nod obediently but his mouth would be watering, his cock hard, and—

Shit. His cock already was hard, right there at the kitchen table in some stranger's dingy apartment.

This was a new low.

He forced his eyes toward the screen of the laptop in front of him. He needed to do some work, enough to justify his day, and then he needed to get the hell out of there. And that night he needed to find someone who'd treat him *right*. That would take care of everything.

IT WAS TAKING TOO LONG for Tristan to come back with Becky. Too long for Trey to sit there staring at the TV, trying to ignore the junior suit, worrying and not able to do a damn thing about it.

He wanted to get up and pace, but that might start Junior talking again, and that wouldn't be good. So far, Trey had managed not to rough the guy up—at least partly because apparently the asshole would *enjoy* it—but if he started in on Becks again Trey didn't think his temper would hold.

Maybe he should just go find Becky himself. Maybe he should have been the one to go after her in the first place. Sure, he'd let himself get dragged into Becky's drama in the past, but that didn't mean he'd do it again. Besides, maybe it hadn't been such a bad thing. Considering what he used to do for a living, Tristan could be kind of uptight about other people having casual sex. But if sex was what made Becky feel better, then what was wrong with giving it to her? And if she was going to bang one of them, it made a hell of a lot more sense for it to be Trey instead of Tristan. Tristan was full-on gay *plus* he was in a relationship. Trey was bi, single, and happy to oblige.

He pushed himself to his feet. "Don't steal anything," he ordered the suit. "Or touch anything. Don't—don't stand up. Just stay right there at that table and do your thing, and somebody'll be back to babysit you soon."

"Where are you going?"

Trey didn't bother to answer, just headed for the door. But he heard something before he got there—quiet voices in the hall,

37

familiar and calm. He whirled and sprinted back to the couch, covering the distance in three giant strides, flopping onto the cushions, fumbling for the remote, and managing to look at least somewhat settled by the time the door opened. He was dimly aware of the suit staring at him, but couldn't do anything about that.

Tristan and Becky came into the living room, his arm around her shoulders. Her face was a bit puffy, but that was all, and when she crossed the room to Trey she sank to the floor beside the couch rather than flopping on top of him. She still leaned back and seemed appreciative of his gentle ruffling of her hair, but she wasn't frantic, not like she'd been earlier. Tristan had fixed her, apparently without sex.

"You want to start touring around tomorrow?" He kept his voice low so the suit wouldn't be able to hear.

"Can we wait that long?"

"There's nothing to give them, yet. No contact info, no flyers." And she needed some sleep. He didn't know what she'd been up to the night before, but she almost always had her spells when she was tired. "You want the couch? You can close your eyes for a bit."

"Yeah," she mumbled, and they silently changed positions. She could have gone over to the other sofa, but it was too short to stretch out on, and lumpy. She was better where she was, and Trey was happy he'd been able to do at least something to help.

He looked over to Tristan, who was standing by the table, watching them, and then saw the junior suit, head bent over his laptop, totally ignoring them—giving them some privacy. He hadn't ratted about Trey's aborted attempt to leave the apartment, and now he was doing what he could to mind his own business.

It wasn't much—just the basics of human decency, really. But it was more than Trey would have expected from the guy. From Seb. That was his name. Seb was maybe a tiny bit less annoying than Trey had thought. Maybe.

Kate Sherwood

Chapter Five

THE REST OF THE DAY WENT fairly smoothly. Seb kept his head and dug into the records he was working through; Tristan helped; Trey and Becky—well, Seb wasn't quite sure what they were doing. Cocooning, it seemed like. Trey was the protective outer layer while Becky was snuggled inside, doing whatever the hell she was doing. Sleeping, mostly, but sometimes waking up and speaking with Trey in low murmurs Seb could almost but not quite interpret.

It was strangely cozy, and when Simon came back in the late afternoon with his list of stores that were willing to serve as information depots, it felt like someone invading the sanctuary. At least, it felt that way to Seb; the others seemed fine with it.

Of course they were; Seb was the invader here, not Simon. That wasn't something to be forgotten.

So he took the information from Simon and packed up his laptop, promised to be back first thing the next morning with photocopied flyers, and left. A quick trip to the office, which was already empty, and he was done for the day.

Back in his Capitol Hill apartment he flipped through photos on his phone, read descriptions, tried to figure out who could give him what he wanted. He had some numbers from guys in the past who'd seemed more than ready to make a repeat engagement, but that was dangerous. Once was fine, but more than that? No, Seb wasn't looking to become dependent on anyone, wasn't looking for a relationship or even a fuck buddy.

He tossed his phone on the couch in disgust. No one tempting. No one who came close to that brief fantasy from earlier in the day, Seb on his knees between Trey's legs…

Damn it, maybe Seb didn't need a random hookup; maybe he just needed to get Trey out of his system. The guy had seemed pretty cozy with Becky, but there'd been something about him that made Seb think a same-sex hook-up wouldn't be a completely foreign territory. And definitely something about him that suggested he'd be fine with the rougher aspects of what Seb was looking for.

Seb had his cell number. There'd been some kerfuffle earlier about whether Trey had minutes on his phone and how important it was that he be reachable and Tristan had insisted on paying for— something. Seb honestly had no idea how the system even worked if you didn't just pay your bill each month. But Tristan had paid, and Simon had made a list of everybody's numbers and distributed it. Seb stared down at his phone, then thumbed through his contacts. There Trey was. No last name. No address. Just ten digits.

It was stupid. It could blow up—it was practically *guaranteed* to blow up. Seb was playing with his reputation, his internship, possibly even his career. This was dangerous.

Hell, yeah. Seb's pulse was already racing as he hit the dial button. He already felt more alive, more truly himself. It was a ten minute drive from his apartment to Tristan's. In ten minutes, Seb could be—oh, fuck, he could be in an alley or something, pressed up against rough brick—

"Yeah?" Trey's voice, gruff and heavy, the greeting sounding more like a challenge.

A challenge Seb suddenly found himself unable to meet. His throat tightened, his heart sped up from "excited" to "terrified" and he sat completely still, eyes fixed on the opposite wall. What was he supposed to say? What was...he knew how to do this with strangers, but someone he kind of knew? Someone he kind of *worked with*?

"Hey!" Trey barked. "You there? Hello, Junior Suit! You hear me?"

Fucking call display. Seb was busted. He needed to do something, say something, come up with—he dropped the phone, then fumbled to pick it up. "Hello?" he said. He sounded almost normal. "Shit, Trey? Sorry, man, butt dial."

There was no response, and Seb pulled his phone away from his head so he could see the screen. Call ended. The fucker had hung up on him. That was that.

Seb stared at the phone. Damn, he was so tempted. He could call back, could say… something, something a hell of a lot better than apologizing for a butt dial. Could he offer to buy Trey a beer to make up for disturbing him? No, that was stupid. Desperate.

And maybe the "desperate" was an accurate description, considering how antsy he was and how much trouble he was having with letting go of this idea. But he couldn't let the "stupid" be true. There were too many people who'd be too disappointed in him if he messed up.

So he flipped through the app on his phone and found a guy who looked almost as rough, almost as built as Trey, and only a couple blocks away.

I need to be taught a lesson, he texted. *You man enough to do it?*

He leaned back into the cushions and waited for the response. It was just another night. And just another kind of stupid. The kind that might get him hurt, but shouldn't get him caught. It was a trade-off he was willing to make.

IT WAS A TRAP. TREY SHOULD have known it. As soon as Becky had left, Simon had disappeared into the bedroom, leaving Trey and Tristan alone. And apparently that had been on purpose.

Now, Tristan stood between Trey and the apartment door,

looking stubborn. Sure, Trey could have barrelled through him without any trouble, but he could never hurt Tristan and Tristan knew it too damn well.

"No," Tristan said now, staring him down. "Not unless you can look me in the eye and tell me you have somewhere to go."

Trey stared back at him. "What?"

"It's raining out. You're not sleeping outside tonight, not in the rain."

"Jesus, it's nothing I haven't done before. It's not like I'll melt."

"It's stupid, though. There's no reason for it. The couch is yours; you know that."

But, no, Trey *didn't* know that, not anymore. "I like the fresh air."

"Open the window."

"Tristan—"

"No. Fuck it. I know things are different now... Simon moved in, Shane's got his own place, Micah's sleeping at Jake's... but you're still welcome here. Especially when it's fucking raining."

"This is Seattle. If I stay every time it rains—"

"It'll be fine. If you stay every night, that's fine."

"No, you want your space."

"You know what I want, now?"

Trey snorted and nodded toward the bedroom wall. "I know what *Simon* wants."

"No, you don't. He hasn't got a problem with you sleeping here. He's not sure how to act, maybe—not sure if he's supposed to be your host, or if that's presumptuous or whatever—but he's got no problem with you staying over. Especially when—"

"Don't tell me about the rain again." Trey didn't like this. The churning, confused feeling that came whenever someone tried to be nice to him. He couldn't let himself be taken in, but more importantly he couldn't let himself be *pitied*. He was Trey: the strong one. If he didn't have that, he had nothing. "I'm good. Thanks for the invitation, but I'm fine."

Tristan frowned. "What about home? Have you talked to them lately? Brent comes and goes, right? If he's not around, your mom wouldn't mind if you—"

"Yeah, good idea. I'll check that out." Trey's voice came out too fast, too loud. Too close to out of control, and Tristan clearly noticed. He stepped aside, leaving a clear path between Trey and the door, and Trey tried not to run as he took the offered escape.

Shit. He made it to the stairway, down half a flight, and then slammed his back against the wall. He was such a loser. A fucking burden, first on his family, then on his friends. Tristan was in love, for the first time ever, and he didn't need some stupid asshole sleeping on his couch, getting in the way of everything. He had enough other shit going on. And it wasn't—it wasn't—what, fair? Wasn't right? It wasn't *good*, in some way that Trey couldn't explain, for Tristan to try to pretend otherwise. To make Trey have to think about it all, make him have to speak the words of his own banishment. Tristan should have just left it all alone and not pretended.

There were noises in the stairwell below and Trey pushed away from the wall and stomped down the stairs. The two people climbing toward him stepped to the side to let him pass and he almost wished they hadn't. It would have felt good to get in a fight with someone. So satisfying to feel his fist connect with something soft and fragile, but fine even the other way around, if someone else was punching him. At least it would have been real, not a lie like the welcome Tristan was trying to—

Trey froze, the sudden realization startling him out of his self-pity.

He didn't *want* to get hit. It didn't turn him on or anything. But the junior suit, with all his polish and his easy way of knowing just what to say to people—maybe he wasn't as different as Trey had been thinking. Maybe he was just looking for something real, himself.

Trey thought about the butt dial. What if it had been something else? A real phone call, made on purpose? What would that have been like?

He stepped out into the drizzle and tried to focus on more immediate concerns. He was too old for the youth shelters, but the few times he'd tried to go to the adult shelters had been—he wasn't sure what they'd been. Sad, he supposed. It was one thing to be in a bit of a mess when you were nineteen or twenty, but something very different to be fifty or sixty and still having to hunt for somewhere safe and dry to sleep. It wasn't anything Trey needed to think about, so he tried to avoid the adult shelters.

Which left him with limited options for the night. And that was fine—he wasn't going to melt if he got a bit wet.

He thought about calling his mom. Brent was her boyfriend, and when he'd moved in he'd made it pretty damn clear it was time for Trey to move out. But as Tristan had said, Brent came and went, and when he was gone Trey's mom could actually be pretty cool. Not a mom-mom—she wasn't baking him cakes or doing his laundry or whatever. But she'd let him sleep on the couch, and let him spend time with his little sisters. He used to babysit them, even, but they were too old to need that, now.

How long had it been since he'd seen them? More than a year. Too damn long. At least, too long for him to go back with his tail between his legs, begging for a spot on the couch just because it was a little rainy out.

No, he wasn't going to do that. He'd catch a bus and sleep while it drove; if the driver wasn't an asshole Trey could be warm and dry for a couple hours like that. Yeah, that was a good plan.

He could stay dry, relax, and while he was at it, he could think about Junior Suit. Sebastian. Think about wanting what was real, and about hitting—no, Trey didn't want to hit him. Not unless he was mad. But pushing him around? What would that be like?

Trey ducked under the roof of the bus shelter and made sure he had his change ready for the fare. Bus drivers didn't like it if you held up the line, and things would go smoother if the driver wasn't pissed off right from the start.

Then he stood there, looked out into the street, and let his mind wander. Yeah, in a different world, maybe the call hadn't been a butt dial. Maybe it had been an invitation. Nothing spelled out, but Seb would have invited Trey over, and he'd have gone. Seb would have a nice apartment, of course, like something on TV. He'd have beer in the fridge, and he'd order in food—Thai. Trey liked Thai. And they'd eat and drink and watch TV, and then when Trey felt like it—Trey, not Sebastian, when *Trey* felt like it— he'd—what? Grab him?

No, it should be slow. No grabbing. Slow, but—what had Seb said?—rough. There was a wrong kind of rough, but there was a right kind, too. A kind Seb had been hoping for.

Trey leaned against the plexiglass wall at the end of the shelter. What was the right kind of rough? His hand in Seb's hair? Tight, maybe pulling a little? Maybe pulling a lot? And guiding his head—well, yeah, guiding it there.

Trey closed his eyes and let himself picture it. Some real emotion on Junior Suit's face, a break in the so-perfect mask. Not fear—Trey didn't want to see fear—but desperation? Or just surrender?

The sounds of the traffic changed and he opened his eyes to see a bus pulling into the space in front of him. His bus, his shelter, at least for a couple hours.

There was no point daydreaming about anything else. No warm, dry apartments, no desperate, pretty preppies. Just this. Trey and the bus.

It was better than being out in the rain. That was what he needed to remember.

Chapter Six

SEBASTIAN PULLED THE FLYERS OUT of his messenger bag and dropped them on Tristan's kitchen table. Becky was already sitting there and she pulled the stack around so she could read them while Tristan peered over her shoulder.

"They look good," he said.

Then a familiar low rumble from behind them. "The flyers?" Seb turned to see—oh, shit. Trey, wearing only jeans, hair still wet from the shower he'd been having when Seb arrived. He had a shirt in his hand but he wasn't rushing to put it on. Was it better that he did, so Seb could preserve at least some measure of his dignity, or that he didn't, so Seb could go on looking at the acres of brown, smooth skin forever? A faint glow spread over the tops of Trey's shoulders, like that was where the water had hit while it was still steaming hot, and Seb's fingers twitched, his whole body aching with eagerness to touch.

The shirt. Fuck. The shirt had to go on. *Please, please, put the shirt on.*

But Trey didn't. He moved closer, as if interested in the flyer, but his eyes flicked to Seb's, once, then twice—was this really happening? Was—was Seb being *invited* to look? To admire?

"Yeah," Tristan said, and edged to the side so there was room for Trey to approach the table. Room enough, even for someone as broad as Trey, but there was still a brush of Trey's bare shoulder against Seb's, and then—oh, Jesus, then the hard muscle of Trey's denim-covered thigh against Seb's hand. Not a brush this time. Trey was just standing there, and his leg was pressed against the back of Seb's fingers as if—

As if it was nothing, which it probably was. This was going too far. Fantasies were one thing, but it was completely unprofessional to let them intrude on reality. Tight space, that was all.

Seb almost squeaked when Becky pushed her chair back more suddenly than he'd been expecting. "Okay," she said, standing up and turning around. "Get dressed," she ordered Trey. "We need to get out there and pass these out, right?"

"That's the plan," Trey said. He stepped backward, away from Seb, and the lost contact was almost enough to throw Seb off balance, to send him stumbling after Trey, falling to his knees—

"And we'll keep researching," Tristan said, just the hint of a question in his tone as he looked at Seb. "We got the skeleton figured out yesterday, but today we need to start putting some meat on it, right?"

Possibly not the best time for someone to say the word 'meat', but Seb fought through it. "Yeah. Okay."

"Shirt," Becky said, glaring at Trey, and then she slapped him, back of her hand into his flat belly. Seb almost sobbed at the sound, the quiver of skin over muscle.

Trey obediently pulled his shirt on, but when his head reappeared through the neck-hole he wasn't looking at Becky, but at Seb. As if he'd known he was being watched. As if he didn't mind, or had even—

"Shoes," Becky barked. "I've got a shift this afternoon—we don't have all day. Let's go!"

It was like one of those internet videos of a kitten chasing a Rotweiller. Trey ducked his head and obediently shuffled away, apparently to look for his shoes, and Tristan divided the stack of flyers roughly into half. Becky found a plastic shopping bag under the sink, slid the flyers into it, and by that time Trey was back, shoes on, ready to go.

For the first time Seb noticed the bags under his eyes. He didn't look exhausted, just tired enough to make Seb wonder about what—or who—had given him a sleepless night. Seb's own evening had been marginally better than the night before, but still clearly not enough to scratch the itch that was making him obsess about Trey. Or maybe it wasn't the lack of a proper fuck that was setting him off, maybe it was the skin, the dark eyes, watching him the way they were now. So it was curiosity? Was that what was going on?

But curious or not, Trey obediently followed Becky out of the apartment without any words in Seb's direction. It should have been a relief, but it somehow wasn't.

"They'll be fine," Tristan said, clearly misinterpreting Seb's preoccupation.

He could go with that. "It's not dangerous?"

"A little, I guess, but nothing Trey can't handle. He's pretty well built—maybe you noticed?"

Seb looked up from the laptop he'd been unpacking and saw Tristan's sly grin. Busted. But apparently it wasn't a big deal. "Kind of hard not to notice," he admitted. "But muscles aren't bullet-proof. Not knife-proof."

"They're both used to it. Trey was living up in The Jungle when he and I met; he knows his way around."

"How long ago was that? I had the impression you guys had been friends for a while, but neither of you is that old…?"

"It's been quite a while. Almost four years, I think? We're both twenty." And then Tristan waited quietly, apparently anticipating more questions.

But Seb wasn't sure if he had any. Tristan and Trey had met when they were sixteen. Trey had been living in the city's most notorious warren of homelessness and poverty, when he was sixteen. Seb had been in France the year he turned sixteen on an international exchange. His whole family had flown over for his birthday.

"What about Becky?" he asked. Trey had shut down the questions the day before, but Tristan seemed more open. "Whatever that was yesterday—could that happen when she's out doing this?"

Tristan shrugged. "I guess. It's not a big deal. She just gets worked up sometimes. Trey can help her out."

"But—what is it? Anxiety, or bipolar, or schizophrenia? Does she have medications that help?"

Tristan's expression was less open, now. "She just gets worked up," he repeated.

"There's nothing wrong with having a mental illness," Seb said. "It's not a big deal."

"That's big of you to say; I'm sure she'll be relieved to hear you're okay with it all."

Shit. Seb was messing this up. "No, I meant—"

"She's fine," Tristan said firmly. "Nothing for you to worry about. Now, you were looking at the corporate registrations yesterday, right? Have you got that spreadsheet ready?"

And the door that had been opened just a little was slammed shut.

Which was—good. It was a bit hard to accept, a little frustrating to realize that the charm that worked on everyone in *Seb's* world didn't seem to work nearly as well here. But, really, if someone had come into Seb's inner circle and started asking nosy questions, he would certainly hope his family and friends would shut things down just as surely as he was being shut down here. "You look after them," he said quietly.

Tristan frowned. "We look after each other."

"Yeah. That's what I meant. It's—I don't know what I was expecting."

"A bunch of savages? Law of the jungle; only the strong survive? Something like that?"

"Not consciously. But subconsciously? I don't know. Maybe."

Tristan didn't seem offended. "Want to hear my treatise on how all the prejudices and bullshit we inflict on each other about race or sexuality or whatever are just a clever smokescreen to cover the true division in our society?"

Seb cocked his head. "Class? Am I sitting in the kitchen of a dreaded socialist?"

"Careful, man. It's contagious."

"I think I'm pretty well inoculated against it."

"Yeah, everyone thinks that. At first." Tristan gave a cartoon-villain laugh and steepled his fingers together in a suitably sinister manner.

Strange how good it felt. Strange how the dinginess Seb had first noticed in this apartment seemed to be—well, certainly not improving, but somehow receding. It wasn't a hovel anymore, it was a home. A home for people Seb genuinely liked, and even respected.

Strange how much had changed in just a couple days.

~*~*~*~

BECKY WASN'T GREAT AT TALKING to people. She tended to get impatient and walk away at the first sign of resistance, but at least she shoved a flyer into their hands before she left. And she hadn't punched anyone in the face yet, which meant she was definitely doing a better job than Trey would have.

So he lurked in the background, out of earshot when she was talking to someone who looked safe, closer when he thought there was something to worry about. He was pretty close most of the time that morning. They were in The Jungle, working through the network of paths between the makeshift shelters various people had made for themselves. Nobody up there could be trusted, not really.

It was pushing noon, the sun sneaking weak rays through the damp, wispy clouds, when she handed him the bag of flyers and said, "I'm done for the day. Gotta work."

"You gonna be able to give me dinner if I come 'round the back?"

She nodded. "Yeah, no problem—Mr. Anderson doesn't mind. I think he thinks it's protection food, kind of. Like if we're feeding you, you won't cause trouble."

Kind of insulting, but Trey didn't care. The restaurant Becky worked at had good food, and free was his favorite price. "Cool."

They walked down the path together and when they reached the road Trey turned to follow Becky but she frowned at him. "It's the middle of the day. You're not going this way, are you? You don't need to walk me."

"It's not like I have anywhere else to be."

"So you have time? You could apply for some more jobs."

He groaned. Becky had been unemployed until a few months earlier and she'd been a hell of a lot easier to take. Now that she had a job she wanted everyone in the world to follow in her footsteps. Like she'd found Job Jesus and wanted to spread the good word.

"I already did that."

"How many places? Like, twenty? That's not enough, Trey!"

"It's enough to know nobody's hiring." At least not hiring people like him. "You were the one who freaked out about me working for Moby, and now you're freaking out 'cause I'm *not* working. Make up your mind, woman."

"I didn't *freak out*. I just—he's not the same, Trey. You know that. Since before the fires, even, he's—he's meaner. He's going to get people hurt, and I don't want you to be one of them."

He wanted to argue with her, but he couldn't. Moby *was* different. Everything was changing. Everything but Trey.

"I'll walk you, and then I'll go into every store in the strip mall and fill out some applications. Okay?"

"You think they're going to hire you at the knitting store?"

"They're not going to hire me anywhere, so what does it matter?"

She didn't look satisfied, but she quit nagging at least, and they walked the rest of the way in peace. And true to his word, Trey went into the knitting store, the make-your-own-beer-and-wine shop, the internet provider storefront and then, with slightly more optimism, the gas station. But the gas station manager said he'd need to see proof of high school graduation before he even handed an application over, so that was that.

It was all pointless. That little bit of fun he'd had that morning, making Sebastian's eyes bug out like they had—it seemed stupid now. Like Trey could ever have any sort of real power over someone like that. Someone all smooth and put together. Someone who was in college, and doing important jobs over the summer. Trey couldn't even get hired at a fucking gas station.

He was heading for The Jungle. He knew it. That was his future. He'd put it off for a while, hanging out with Tristan and the rest of them, but they'd just been killing time, building their strength. Slumming, just for a bit, but now they were moving up. Fuck, even Shane had a job and a boyfriend. Trey? He had nothing.

He saw the sedan at the side of the road beneath the overpass and ignored it. No, that wasn't quite right. He was aware of it, knew that it was potentially a bad situation, something he shouldn't walk into, but he just didn't give a shit. So when he reached the car and three guys stepped out, two blocking his path while the third circled in behind him, he wasn't surprised, exactly. No, this was just the next logical step.

Still, he shouldn't be stupid about it, so he raised his hands out to the sides and said, "Sorry, guys, I'm fucking broke. I got nothing worth taking."

"We don't want your shit," the tallest one said. He wasn't quite as solid as Trey, but he was taller so he'd have a better reach. And there were two others to worry about. Nah, Trey wasn't going to fight his way out of this one.

And he sure wasn't going to be able to talk his way out, so he just stood there and waited to see what happened next.

"What's in your little bag, there?" the tall one asked. "You been trick-or-treating a bit early?"

Someone else would have been able to come up with a smart-ass reply, but Trey wasn't a quick thinker. Not a thinker at all. So he reached into the bag and pulled out a flyer. "You want one?"

"I've already got one," the man said. "You think you're going to turn people into fucking *spies*? You think we haven't already got that covered? You think we didn't know what you were doing the second you stepped out the door of that shithole apartment?"

The sweat on Trey's skin turned cold. This wasn't random. These fuckers had been watching him? Watching *Becky*, and the rest of the gang? They knew where Tristan lived.

A car drove by and honked its horn. What was the point of that? Did it not like the parking job, or had the driver seen there was something bad going on and decided that a fucking honked horn would be his part in helping to solve the problem?

Still, maybe it was a useful reminder. "It's the middle of the day," Trey said. "People are watching."

"Get in the car. We'll find somewhere quieter to talk."

Trey shook his head. "All I've got to say is 'fuck you' and I can say that just fine right here."

The tall one stepped forward and Trey could sense the other two shifting behind him, blocking his escape.

He let his instincts take over. No backing up, not for him. He charged forward, low and fast, and felt the satisfying thud of his shoulder driving into the tall guy's belly. They both staggered, but Trey stayed on his feet and kept moving, jumping, his boots smashing onto the hood of the car, then the impact against the pavement as he leapt off into the road. Another blaring horn but Trey just kept running.

When he hit the opposite sidewalk he glanced back and saw one of the men halfway across the road, the tall one behind the driver seat, and the third standing uselessly on the sidewalk.

God, it was tempting to stop running. To turn and yell an insult, or better yet wait for the guy who was crossing the road to catch up and then take him on. But it would soon turn into three-to-one, so... no. If Shane had been there, it would have been worth the chance. The two of them against the other three? Maybe they'd have lost, but it would have been a hell of a fight.

And it would have suited Trey's temperament a lot better than running.

He took another look behind him, saw no one following, and slowed to a jog, then a walk. He still had to be careful, but he had time. So he pulled his phone out, glad he had minutes, and hit Tristan's number.

"They're watching the apartment," Trey said as soon as he heard Tristan's voice. No time for chit-chat. "They knew what we were doing—me and Becks. She's at work, but we need to make sure she stays there until we can pick her up. Three guys tried to jump me, or at least scare me. They definitely wanted to send us a message."

"Are you safe now?"

"Yeah. Probably."

"Do you need someone to come get you?"

As if Trey needed protection. Trey was the *protector.* "I'm fine. Call Shane and tell him we need to talk. I'm on my way to your place."

"Call when you're close and we'll watch for you."

Trey hung up without agreeing. They could watch for him all they wanted, but if he got in trouble they absolutely needed to stay inside the apartment and just *watch.* They couldn't risk themselves, not for someone useless like Trey.

But he wouldn't be useless, not if he could keep the others safe. So that was what he needed to do. He wouldn't let anything get in the way.

Chapter Seven

IT WAS HARD TO ACCEPT. Not the story itself—at Simon's insistence, Trey had gone over the details several times, and there was never anything about it that made Seb think Trey was lying, or even exaggerating. More like the opposite, probably, playing down the danger he'd been in.

No, the part that was hard to accept was that Seb was somehow involved in all this. He'd taken a summer job that would look good on a resume and might make him some connections, and somehow ended up working in this dingy apartment with people who were apparently under surveillance by a criminal organization, people who were accosted on the street and didn't immediately phone the police... people who, in Trey's case, *still* didn't seem to think they should phone the police.

"It's not like they're going to do anything," Trey said from the spot by the window he seemed to like so much.

Tristan shook his head. "We need to at least give them the chance."

"You can call if you want, but I'm not talking to them." Trey sounded like a sulky little boy, which was strangely endearing. Damn, Seb was not thinking straight about this guy.

Tristan was more hard-headed. "Trey, it's their job to keep Becky and everyone else safe. If you don't tell them what they need to know, they can't do their job."

"They're not going to do their job anyway!"

"If they don't, that's on them. But if you don't even tell them, and then something bad happens? Then it'll be on you."

"It's a waste of time," Trey said, but there was something in his tone that made it clear to everyone that he was giving in.

Which apparently made Tristan decide to move on to the next challenge. "While we're at it—you can't sleep rough anymore, not until we have this figured out. You need to stay here."

"What? No, that's—"

"Absolutely necessary," Simon said firmly. He and Tristan exchanged a look that made Seb's stomach twist—there was such trust in it, appreciation and affection and everything else. Teamwork had never seemed sexy before, but it sure did now. "You're far too vulnerable sleeping outside, or even at a shelter."

"And we need you to be healthy and strong," Tristan added.

It was a compelling presentation, but Seb was pretty sure the teamwork actually made Trey *less* likely to want to stay in the apartment. It would have been bad enough to impose on a friend, but to intrude into this perfect couple, who were actually displaying their perfection even as they tried to arrange the intrusion? Seb would have hated it as well.

Still, he surprised himself a little when he said, "I've got a spare bedroom." It was true enough—his parents had bought the condo for him as an investment, and hadn't worried too much about the extra cost since they were expecting it to increase in value. But why the hell had he brought it up? Did he actually want Trey in his home?

Yeah, he realized. He did. And not as a sexual thing—that was actually an added complication, not a bonus. He just—he wanted to help. He *was* part of this, somehow, and that meant he wanted to be sure he was on the right side of it all. "I'd feel safer," he said. "I mean, if they're watching this apartment, they could have followed me home to mine too, right? It's got a pretty good security system, I guess, but it's not foolproof. If people are buddying up, I need a buddy."

Three sets of eyes stared at him in disbelief, and he was kind of insulted. "What? I'm not supposed to be safe?"

The silence stretched for quite a while before Trey finally said, "You're supposed to *quit*."

"What?"

"This isn't what you signed up for." Tristan sounded almost as confused as Trey had. "You've got a life to go back to—school, and your family, and all that good stuff. You're not—we don't expect you to stick around for this. Not if it's getting dangerous."

65

"It's been dangerous from the start. The foundation only got involved because people were killed—maybe those deaths weren't completely deliberate, but they were careless enough that they may as well have been. I knew what I was getting into."

"No, you didn't." Trey's voice was soft enough that it felt like a reminder, not a contradiction.

Seb frowned at him. He wanted to object, but— "Yeah. Okay. I didn't." He hadn't known he was going to actually *like* these people. Hadn't known he was going to care about what happened to them. "But too bad. I'm in now. I'm not quitting. And I've got a spare bedroom and I'd be happy to have you use it."

Trey's frown hadn't eased. "You don't want that. You don't want to mix your worlds."

Jesus, when had this guy—this fucking goon, this sullen, muscle-bound loser—gotten so perceptive? "It's okay," Seb said. "My apartment—it's not really part of my other world. It's just for me." Just for him and the rough fucks he brought home. He visited his friends and family in their homes or in public places, not his condo. And then, even though he'd rather not have to say it in front of an audience, he added, "I'm not trying to pick you up or try anything sleazy—there's a lock on the bedroom door."

The frown faded. "You honestly think I need a lock to keep you in line?"

Jesus. *To keep you in line.* Seb's mouth was suddenly dry and he didn't trust himself to speak.

"It'd be great," Tristan said, filling the silence before it became too horribly awkward. "Becky's living at home, but you know how that goes—she'll need somewhere to crash if she gets in a fight with them, so it'd be good if the couch was open here. I think Amanda's a bit freaked out about all of this, so it might be good if she just stayed clear. Then Shane could watch Noah, Jake and Micah could buddy-up—it'd just be the two of you left to worry about. If you can keep an eye on each other, we're all good."

"You'd need to be careful *all the time*," Trey said with a frown in Seb's direction. "This isn't a game. If you go—I don't know, go visit your friends or whatever—you need to be careful then, too, without me around."

"You don't think my friends would be enough protection?"

Trey snorted. "I doubt it."

"A different kind of protection," Tristan said thoughtfully. "They're more respectable than us, right? They have families who'd make a fuss if something happened to them, just like you do."

Seb nodded slowly. It was true—he couldn't imagine what hell his parents would unleash on anyone who dared to touch either of their children—but it wasn't necessarily useful. If Seb wasn't in danger, then Trey had no reason to stay in his guest room, and that meant *Trey* would be in danger. Which simply wasn't acceptable. "I don't think we've got a crystal clear idea of who we're dealing with. It'd be nice to assume they were that practical, that professional, but I'm not sure we can. So, yeah, my family would make a hell of a fuss, and so would my friends' families, but that doesn't necessarily mean the people we're facing are smart enough to leave us alone."

"Maybe we should *let* them mess with you." Trey's expression was cool. "If that's what it takes to make people care. Some junkies get burned up and it's no big deal, but god forbid anyone mess with a fine young citizen like you."

"I'm committed to the cause," Seb responded, "but not quite *that* committed."

Trey grinned at him. A real smile, sweet and warm, and Seb felt his shoulders lower as they released tension he hadn't even known he'd been carrying. Trey had been kidding; he hadn't really wanted to sacrifice Seb just to get public attention. Such a small thing, but apparently it meant a lot, at least to Seb's shoulders.

"Okay, then." Trey pushed away from the window as if suddenly energized. "I'll be your bodyguard. But we've got to make sure Becks is safe before we go anywhere, and I need to talk to Shane at some point pretty soon. We need to try to figure out how else they're going to be coming at us."

"And you'll have a better idea of that if we can figure out who the hell we're dealing with," Seb said. "We need to keep at the research."

"Good." Simon looked at his watch. "Tristan, can you call the police and see if someone will come over to take Trey's statement? And we've got a couple hours of good reading time before someone has to go get Becky—might as well get to it."

Trey didn't move from his post at the window, so apparently he still wasn't interested in the research side of things. But he also didn't stop Tristan from phoning the police. Seb and Simon and Tristan fell back into their pattern of reading pretty quickly. Trey stared out the window, mostly, occasionally going for what could only be described as a *prowl* around the apartment. He should have been a distraction, and in some ways he was. But he was also a comfort, a solid, reassuring strength between Seb and the outside world. Trey had said he'd be Seb's bodyguard; Seb was willing to take him up on the offer.

The police eventually arrived and took Trey's terse, sullen statement. Seb wished—what, exactly? He wished he had permission, he supposed. Permission to touch, to sooth and cajole. If Becky had been there she would have snuggled up next to Trey and softened him a little, and the police would have gotten a better impression. As it was, the officers seemed about as impatient with the situation as Trey himself was, and it looked like Trey's prediction of inaction was a self-fulfilling prophecy. He was acting like he didn't care, so why should the police act like *they* cared?

It was frustrating. Simon walked the officers to the door, which was something, at least; Simon would make sure they were aware of the larger context and were paying attention to the safety of *everyone,* rather than just Trey. But Seb?

Seb was close enough to see this all happening, but too distant to be able to do anything about it. So was he any use at all?

He turned his attention back to his laptop. Research. Sorting through the maze of shell corporations, trying to find the people behind the crimes. *That* was what he could do. And the faster he did it, the safer people would be. Even the ones who were too damn stubborn to admit they needed help.

Chapter Eight

SEB'S APARTMENT WASN'T AS NICE as Trey had expected. It was pretty clearly expensive—the neighborhood, the size, the windows and brick, the luxury kitchen and bathrooms—but it wasn't *nice*, not in the way he'd thought it would be. The furniture was probably high-end, but there wasn't much of it, and the posters on the wall? Yeah, they were framed and everything, but they were for bands Trey had heard of, movies he'd seen. There was a dishwasher that likely cost more than some people's cars, but that didn't mean there weren't dishes in the sink, and when Seb offered Trey a beer he handed it over in a bottle, not a fancy glass.

And it was a damn Budweiser.

Trey stood there in the fancy kitchen, lifted the bottle to the light, and peered skeptically through the familiar brown glass. "Is this a trick?"

Seb looked almost defensive. "It's just a beer, not a damn statement."

"Yeah, but... Bud?"

"You want something different? I've got a couple bottles of wine—"

"No. This is great." Trey took a hearty swig to prove his enthusiasm. Despite the reassuring words, he was almost surprised to find the familiar light taste flowing over his tongue. It was a Bud; from a bottle, sure, but still a Bud. He swallowed, then said, "You serve this to your friends?"

"I told you—my apartment isn't part of that world."

"So even before you started hanging out with us, you had— you had a Bud world, and a regular world?"

"Jesus, do you think you might be over-emphasizing the beer a little?"

"If you served this to your friends, what would they say?"

Seb looked like he was planning a lie, but finally he shrugged. "They'd think I was joking, I expect. But that's on me. It's not because they're snobs, it's because I—I go along with stuff. They like—okay, yeah, they like the kind of beer you're expecting them to like. Craft stuff, microbreweries or whatever. They genuinely *like* it. They're not being fake."

"But *you're* being fake? When you drink that stuff?"

Seb snorted and lifted his own bottle to his lips. When he was done drinking he said, "You're a roommate, not a psychologist."

Well, Trey was thinking of himself more as a bodyguard than a roommate, but they definitely agreed about what he *wasn't*. "So—" So, what? What were they supposed to talk about? Maybe nothing. "That's my room, you said? I guess I should go settle in.

Thanks for the beer." And thanks for breakfast in the morning, because Trey didn't have the money for either groceries or eating out. But he'd worry about that when the time came.

"You don't have to hide out in there. I mean, if you want to watch TV or something—" Seb stopped talking long enough to run a hand through his hair, and as his arm lifted Trey watched for clues about what his body was like under the fabric of his dress shirt. Not too built, but definitely not fat. Fit, probably, lots of lean preppy muscle like a rower or a tennis player or something.

Trey took a quick swallow of his beer. Best not to think about the body. "TV?" he managed. Then he looked at Seb's face for the first time in a while, and the bruise he'd gotten used to seeing suddenly looked darker, fresher. "You don't have plans already? That guy?"

Seb raised his hand and touched his cheek as if checking whether the mark still hurt. "Not him, no. He was just a one-time thing."

"You let someone you don't know do that to you? What the hell were you thinking?"

"I was thinking I wanted to get off." Seb's jaw was thrust out like he was daring Trey to comment on that, daring him to judge. When Trey didn't take the bait, Seb's face relaxed a little and he shrugged. "It didn't work out too well."

"Aren't there—I mean, it's not my thing, so I don't know— Tristan might, if you wanted some help—aren't there clubs or something for—for people like you?"

Seb sighed. "I don't want to join a club. I don't want to *perform* my sexuality. Does that makes sense to you? All the leather and toys and rituals—that's not what I'm into."

"So you've tried it?" Trey was being nosy, but Seb could tell him to fuck off if he didn't want to answer the questions. And it kind of seemed like he actually *wanted* to talk about it, so... why not ask?

"Yeah, a couple times. Not here. I was in London last year and there's a pretty active scene over there. But—" He frowned and leaned back against the polished stone counter. "You actually want to hear about all this?"

"Sure, yeah. Why not? Tristan used to tell us some of the crazier stuff his clients got into. Most of it was kinda gross, but some of it?" It was Trey's turn to shrug. "I could see how people got off on some of it."

"So Tristan really was a prostitute? I mean, he'd said a couple things that made me wonder, but—that's for real? And it's okay to just talk about it? It's not a secret or anything?"

Oh, shit, maybe it *was* a secret. Trey wasn't sure. "I guess—I mean, don't go advertising it. But you told me about your weird sex stuff, so—"

"So it's okay for you to tell me about *Tristan's*?" There was something new in Seb's gaze, something Trey found unsettling, but not necessarily in a bad way. "Shouldn't you be telling me *your* secrets, not someone else's?"

"I don't have any secrets. I'm an open book."

"*No* secrets? Bullshit."

Trey spread his arms out to the sides. "What you see is what you get."

"I bet I can find some secrets," Seb said. He turned and pulled the fridge door open, then bent a little to fish inside for two new bottles of beer. "If I ask you questions—just about sex stuff, not anything totally personal—I bet I can find something you don't want the whole world to know."

"I don't want the whole world to know any damn thing about me. Not even my name." Trey drank the last of his beer and let Seb take the empty in exchange for a full bottle.

"You never do anything at all kinky? No, like—I don't know, no role playing or fuzzy handcuffs or any of that totally safe stuff?"

"I fuck girls sometimes. I think that's about as weird as I get."

"Because you want to? Like, you're bisexual? Or just because they want you to and you're too much of a pushover to say 'no' to them?"

"You think I'm a pushover?"

"I think Becky could tell you to light your hair on fire and you'd be reaching for the matches."

Well, Becky. Yeah, okay, Becky. "I've fucked other girls, not just her. Because—yeah, I guess because I wanted to."

"But you like fucking guys, too."

"Yeah, sure."

Seb grinned. "You seem to have a somewhat reversed idea of what the default preference should be. Most people would consider it kinky for you to fuck guys, not girls."

Trey shrugged. He wasn't too interested in what most people thought.

"So, bisexual—interesting, but clearly not a secret. But maybe there's something else? Not necessarily something you've *done*, but something you've thought about? Like, when Tristan was telling you stories about his clients and some of it was interesting—what kind of stuff sounded good?"

Well, that was—was it a secret? Not really, just awkward in the current circumstances. "I don't know—some of the stuff—I mean, I never want to hurt anybody. I like fighting and I like fucking, but I don't want the two of them combined. But, like..." Jesus, was he actually going to talk about this? To Seb? He took a deep swallow of his beer. "He had a guy who would never talk to him. Like, not a single word, not even orders. He'd just—like, if he wanted Tristan's shirt off, he'd just turn Tristan around and unbutton his shirt and take it off. If he wanted Tristan to lie a certain way, he'd just move him around. Like Tristan was a doll or something. Turns out the guy was from the Middle East somewhere and didn't actually speak much English, so part of it was just that he *couldn't* use words. But he was a rich guy, lots of people who could have taught him, and Tristan worked for him for, like, a couple years. If he'd wanted to learn the words he could have. He just didn't want to."

"And that seemed hot to you?" There was a new note in Seb's voice, a slight huskiness that made Trey aware of how his own throat felt tighter than usual. "Did you imagine yourself doing that?"

Trey shrugged and tried to sound casual. "I guess, yeah. Maybe."

"Were you the doll, or the man playing with the doll?"

"Not the doll."

"So you like being in control."

"I guess." Trey swallowed hard and saw Seb's eyes track the movement.

"And you like imagining things. At least sometimes." Seb wasn't asking, now, not with his voice, but there was a question in his gaze, absolutely. He stepped closer and spoke in a lower voice. "The other day, after I told you about the guy getting too rough with me—did you imagine anything around that? Like maybe what it would be like to be in his place? How you'd handle it better than he did?"

"Yeah. I thought about it a bit."

Seb stepped closer. "And this morning, when you were walking around half-naked… was that for me? At least a little?"

A long swallow of beer. "Maybe a little."

Seb was somehow closer, almost too close to keep pretending they were just talking. His eyes were hot and bright on Trey's. "And just now, when I bent over to pull the beers out of the fridge—did you think about keeping me bent over? Think about what you could do to me in that position."

If he was going to be honest, Trey hadn't gotten quite that far. "I'm thinking about it now."

"Yeah?" Seb smiled, lifted his bottle to his lips and kept his gaze steady on Trey's as he drank. "Anything you'd like to share with the class?"

There was a moment when it all seemed inevitable. Trey wasn't sure exactly what would happen—well, he wasn't sure exactly *how* it would happen—but obviously it would. Of course it would.

Seb didn't even move his feet, but something in his body changed, as if he was leaning forward, or somehow drawing Trey in toward him. Trey knew just how Seb's hair would feel, gripped tight in Trey's fist, as if he'd held him before. As if they'd done this before.

But that was crazy, and Trey didn't want any more crazy in his life.

He stepped—stumbled—backward, away from Seb and all the temptation in his wide eyes. "I'm tired. I should sleep."

Damn it, the expression on Seb's face wasn't fair. He had no right to look confused, or betrayed, or whatever the hell it was that was tugging at Trey. It had been a come on, and Trey had done the smart thing by turning it down, and that was all.

He forced himself to turn and head for the guest bedroom. Once he was inside, he shut the door behind him and leaned against it like he needed his weight to hold it shut.

Like he needed to make sure he didn't accidentally open it again.

Seb had just been looking for a fuck, and Trey had been handy. That was all. Shit, if Trey stayed in his room, maybe Seb would call someone else, or go out himself and find someone to give him what he wanted.

Trey could have been that guy, at least for one night. He could have *taken care* of Seb, made sure that he got off without getting hurt. But Trey had freaked out. Chickened out.

Shit.

He took a deep breath and held it. In the silence he heard something scuffle, something moving just outside the bedroom door. Seb. Doing what?

Another deep breath, then Trey stepped away from the door, turned, and pulled it open.

~*~*~*~

SEB FROZE, HIS HAND HOVERING in the air over the door that was no longer in front of him. "I was going to knock," he said quickly. He wasn't sure if it was true, but he'd give himself the benefit of the doubt. He might have chickened out, but he might not have. "I wanted to apologize for making it weird. My mom would kick my ass if she knew I was being such a shitty host. I'm sorry. I shouldn't have dragged you into my crap."

Trey's expression was unreadable. After a moment he said, "The other night, when you called me. Was that really a butt dial?"

He might as well get it over with. "No. Sorry for that, too."

"Sorry for calling? Or for not saying anything?"

Excellent damn question, and one it would have been a lot easier to answer if Seb was able to find any emotions in Trey's face or body. "In terms of an apology, I guess I'm sorry for calling. In terms of regrets?" He shrugged. "I don't know, to be honest."

"You don't know." Trey licked his lips, and there was a flicker of something in his eyes that gave Seb hope. Uncertainty. Excitement. Something that meant Trey was feeling *something*, at least. Then Trey reached out his hand and brought it, ever so slowly, to Seb's face. His touch was gentle, his fingers cupping Seb's jaw, up over his cheekbone, and Seb wanted to groan in frustration. All the buildup, the stupid risk, and this was all he was going to get out of it. Something soft and gentle and—

Trey's thumb found the bruise on Seb's cheek and pushed on it. Hard.

Seb's gasp was shaky, half pain and half arousal, and his eyelids fell shut as if they were weighted. He let his head tilt back under the pressure from Trey's hand and stood there with his throat naked and exposed.

"Don't play," Trey said, his voice a low rumble that ran through Seb's entire body. "You said you don't want to perform, so don't. If you say stop, I'm going to stop. So don't say it if you don't mean it. Clear?"

"Yeah," Seb said. He was tempted to throw a "sir" in there, but maybe that'd be the kind of performance he'd said he didn't want and that Trey didn't seem interested in, either.

Trey's free hand tugged at Seb's shirt, dragging it out of his waistband then up over his head, but not all the way off. Seb dragged at his arms impatiently, trying to free himself, only to feel the pressure on his bruise increase.

"No," Trey scolded. Fuck, yeah, he *scolded*. "Turn around."

Seb did as he was told, deliciously aware of how vulnerable he was, with his hands still caught in his shirt. And it all got just a little more intense when he felt Trey twisting the fabric, not freeing Seb but tightening his bonds.

Then Trey's broad, strong body pressed up against Seb, Seb's arms hanging useless behind him, his hands—oh, god, his hands brushing against the hardness of Trey's cock through rough denim. His fingers curled instinctively, hunting for a grip, but Trey caught him and pulled his hands up to the middle of his back.

"Not until you're told." Then Trey pulled their bodies together, one arm around Seb's chest, fingers pulling and pinching his nipple, the other hand jerking at Seb's belt, then his fly, then digging past his underwear and wrapping around his cock. His grip was tight, confident, like he was just taking what was his, and Seb felt himself relax. Not his body—it was still coiled tight in anticipation. But his brain let go. He didn't need to think about any of this. Trey was in charge. Trey would do whatever he wanted and it didn't matter what Seb wanted, so there was no point even worrying about any of that. He was free to let himself float and to just *feel* it all.

And that was what he did. He felt Trey's rough grip, felt his stubble and the blessing of his teeth against the sensitive skin of Seb's throat, felt his pants being tugged down, his body bent and rearranged, and then the coolness of spit and the blunt pressure of Trey's cock.

Seb's body surrendered almost too quickly, before the pain was more than discomfort. Trey's cock was thick and long and there should have been more of a fight, more of a struggle. But Seb's body knew what it wanted as surely as his mind did, and Trey slid deep, slid *home*, easily.

The rhythm after that was a punishing reward. Too hard and fast to speak, to think, to do anything but fight for balance and let himself go. Seb's body was contorted, his head pulled back by Trey's firm grip on his hair, his back arched, his ass stretching and fighting for more. His orgasm was just one more sensation, one more pleasure, one more announcement that he'd found perfection.

His body sagged when the last wave washed through him but Trey didn't let him fall. A few more thrusts, a deep, growling grunt that sent a rush of blood to Seb's spent cock, and then Trey straightened, peeling his sweat-sticky skin away, easing his grip on Seb's hair.

"That okay?" Trey asked.

Seb turned his laugh of surprise into a cough. "Yeah, good," he managed eventually. "Okay for you?"

He turned in time to see Trey frowning as if he actually had to think about the answer. Not too flattering—Seb had just had the best fuck of the year, and Trey was having to find a diplomatic way to say it hadn't worked for him?

Instead, though, Trey said, "You like it like that? I mean—I just did whatever I felt like. I barely thought of you at all."

Seb tidied himself a little and did up his fly. The apartment had its own laundry room, thank god. "That's the point," he finally said. "I don't *want* people to think about me. Not—" He stopped. "I don't actually like analyzing it. I don't feel like I should have to. Like, people who get all worked up about whether being gay is nature or nurture or whatever? It feels like people are looking for an excuse, and I don't think I should *need* a fucking excuse. Not for being gay, not for liking what I like. It's just the way I am, and if you don't like it that's your problem, not mine."

"I never said I didn't like it." Trey sounded cautious, but also amused. "Worked out pretty well for me, really." He'd pulled his own pants up at some point but his chest was still bare, and Seb wanted to reach out and run his fingers over the hairless skin…

But that wasn't what this was about. Fucking, not cuddling. "Okay, then. Everybody's happy. I have to go to the office for a bit tomorrow morning; if you want I can go there on my own so you can sleep in, and then I'll swing back around and pick you up before I go to the dangerous land."

Trey frowned. "You think nobody can mess with you on this side of town? This is where all the trouble is *coming from*, you know. The whole point of my sleeping here is because they could find you here, right?"

"Yeah, okay, but—" But what? What was Seb's argument here, one that didn't blow the whole I-need-protection-so-you're-doing-*me*-a-favor line?

He obviously took too long to think. "Don't worry," Trey said, and his voice was hard again, like it had been when they'd first met. "I won't go inside with you at your office. You can park down the block if you want and I'll just trail along behind you and make sure you're okay until you get inside. Nobody needs to see us together."

"I don't—" Well. It *wasn't* what Seb had been thinking, not entirely. It wouldn't be that hard for him to explain Trey's presence at the office; it was his *job* to be working with Trey and his gang, after all. But it likely wasn't a bad thing for Trey to be a little mad at him. It wouldn't be good to get too cozy, or make him think the two of them were something they weren't. They'd fucked, that was all. Just one more in a long string of fucks for both of them. Nothing important. It didn't matter if Trey thought Seb was a snob; it was *good* if he thought that. So Seb made himself shrug. "Okay," he said. "That sounds good. I'll want to leave here around eight thirty—can you set an alarm for yourself or do you want me to wake you up?"

"I can manage," Trey said, all prickles and wounded pride, and it shouldn't have made Seb's stomach twist so unpleasantly. It shouldn't have mattered at all what Trey thought, not about any of it. That wasn't what this was about.

"Okay," Seb said. "Great. So I'll see you tomorrow morning." He turned and headed for his room. When he reached his doorway he turned and looked across the living room to the other short hall, expecting to see Trey still standing there, watching. But Trey was gone, the door to his room already closed.

Trey wasn't going to be sending longing looks after Seb; that wasn't his style. And that was good. It was excellent. Seb had made a smart choice. He'd gotten a great fuck, and he'd sleep well, and that was all that mattered. No need for regrets.

That was what he told himself. But when he shut the door he leaned against it and listened for a while, hoping to hear some sort of movement, something he could use as an excuse to go back out and make things better.

But there was no noise. Trey was probably asleep already, the selfish bastard.

Seb shook his head at his own nonsense and headed for his bathroom. He'd shower, he'd sleep, and he'd wake up with a better attitude.

One that kept him from worrying what some one-time fuck thought about him. One that could keep a better grip on the annoying whispers trying to fight their way to the top of his brain. One that let him forget about Trey's strength, his solidity, his real-ness.

Seb hadn't been looking for anything more than a fuck, and he'd gotten what he wanted. He was done. He just needed to make sure he remembered that.

Chapter Nine

TREY WOKE UP CONFUSED. Where the hell was he? Why was it so soft, so warm… oh. It all came back to him. The big bed, the private bathroom with the crazy rainfall shower head, the coffee he could smell seeping in from the next room—he'd earned it all. He'd given the rich boy what he wanted, and gotten some comfort in return.

Well, fuck it, Trey had made worse deals in his life.

He swung his legs out of bed and reached for his phone. Still five minutes before his alarm would go off, so he didn't have to get up right away, but there was no point letting himself get used to the good life.

Still, there was no point in being stupid about things, so he let himself lie on the plush rug on the floor to do his sit ups and push ups and all the other exercises he'd figured out as a way to keep himself strong without a fancy gym, and he spent a little extra time in the shower with the weight of the water feeling like a massage on his burning muscles.

It felt strange to pull his clothes on before leaving the bedroom—after the night before, was he really going to worry about showing a bit of skin? But Seb had obviously wanted to make it clear there were boundaries between them; fucking hadn't meant anything, hadn't changed anything. So Trey would show he understood that and wasn't *looking* for more, not from a stuck-up little preppy like Seb.

He stalked out to the kitchen in jeans and a Henley, but Seb wasn't anywhere in sight. The coffee was on—but it looked like a pretty fancy machine, so there was almost certainly a timer.

Seb was still asleep. Trey was alone.

It felt strange.

He practically tiptoed into the living room and stood in the middle of the floor, looking around. There were no personal touches; did Seb even *like* the movies displayed on his framed posters? No pictures of family or even of Seb himself. No books, no knickknacks or souvenirs. There was a cushion on the floor as if it had been dropped and not tidied up, a few pieces of clothing strewn around—enough to make the place feel lived in, but not enough to make it feel like a home.

Not that Trey was any kind of expert on what homes should feel like.

He padded back to the kitchen, the hardwood floor cool beneath his bare feet, and poured himself a cup of coffee, even though he didn't like it much. He looked in the fridge but didn't find anything that looked like a meal. And then he sat there at the breakfast bar and wondered how much it had cost to make the wooden kitchen table look as battered and rustic as it did.

Seb stumbled out of his room a few minutes later, wearing plaid flannel sleep pants that looked ragged enough to be old favorites, and no shirt. So he wasn't worrying too much about boundaries, maybe, except when he saw Trey he froze and then actually stepped back in apparent surprise.

"Am I not supposed to be here?" Trey asked. Had he misunderstood the setup, somehow?

"No, sorry, I just—I forgot." Seb's hair was ruffled up and there was a crease from his pillow running down the side of his face. He blinked his eyes like an owl exposed to daylight, then rubbed the back of his neck with both hands. "Wow. Yeah, I totally forgot you were here."

"Are you always this slow in the mornings, or did you get a brain injury overnight?"

Seb huffed out something that sounded like a laugh. "No, I'm—I'm usually a bit slow, but not this bad. I just—I slept really well, I guess. Like, I was out of it. Sorry."

"If your bed's anywhere near as nice as mine, I'm surprised you don't sleep really well *every* night." Trey slid off the stool he'd been perched on. "You want me to get you some coffee? I could leave you to do it yourself, but I'm afraid you'd pee in a mug and pour the coffee down the toilet."

"Sure, yeah. Thanks. Just milk, please." Seb smiled and seemed to be waking up. "I don't think I have much to offer for breakfast. I usually just make oatmeal."

"I'd offer to make that, but I have no idea how."

"You don't know how to make oatmeal?"

"Not much of a cook." Trey lifted the carton of milk above the newly poured mug of coffee and said, "Tell me when."

It was all more relaxed than Trey had expected. Absolutely casual and friendly. Seb's groggy start had been a gift, blurring them right through any potential awkwardness. Now they puttered around in the kitchen, Seb making oatmeal, Trey watching with mild interest, and it was fine. Sure, Trey's eyes kept wandering to the purple spot he was pretty sure his teeth had left on Seb's shoulder, but that was just curiosity. And maybe he kind of wanted to reach out and touch it, maybe wanted to press on the mark like he'd pressed the other asshole's bruise the night before, wanted to see if Seb would react as perfectly to this bit of pain as he had to the other—

Shit.

"I'll get my stuff packed up," he said quickly. "And then you have to go to your office? I can wait outside, okay?"

"You can come in to the office," Seb said. "It's fine. And you're not packing up *all* your stuff, are you? You'll be here again tonight, so you can leave most of it."

"You—you want me here again? Another night?"

Seb frowned. "Not for—I mean, I don't know about *sex*, but sleeping? Yeah, you're supposed to be sleeping here until we know it's safe, right?"

Trey shook his head. "Until we know it's safe? We didn't think that through. This is a long-term thing, here. Like, we don't know how long it's going to take to figure all this out, we don't know when it's going to get better." *We don't know* if *it's going to get better.* "You can't have me staying here that whole time. You've got a life to get on with. And if you're looking for a roommate, you need to find one who can pay rent, which isn't me. Seriously, man—I think when you go to the office today, you should just stay there. Don't go back over to Tristan's. This isn't your fight. It's not something you want to be changing your whole life over."

"We already covered this."

"Not enough. Seriously, you think I'm going to stay here for the whole four months you're supposed to be working with us? Nah." Not that Trey would have minded, but he needed to be realistic about the situation. "You've got a sweet setup here. No roommate on purpose, right? So you don't want to blow that now."

"No roommate because—because it would get in the way. I want to be able to—you know, to invite guys over—"

"I get it," Trey said quickly. "I don't need the details." Didn't *want* the details of Seb hooking up with other guys, guys who might hurt him more than he wanted them to.

"And because I didn't want to explain it," Seb said. "Didn't want someone I knew asking me questions or—or even just *knowing* that about me. It's not that I'm ashamed, exactly. Like I said last night, this is how I am and I'm not apologizing. But it's private, you know?"

"I guess that'd make more sense to me if you hadn't told *me* all about it at the first chance you got."

Seb shook his head. "Yeah, that was—I don't know what that was. A mistake, technically."

Technically. What the hell was that supposed to mean? Well, it didn't matter. "So the point is, you've got a system worked out and it's going good, so you don't want me hanging around and messing it up."

"Hey, Trey?" Seb's voice was quiet, but somehow it still caught Trey's attention. "When we're messing around—if we ever do again, I mean—that's when you can tell me what I want. But any other time? I'll make my own decisions, thanks."

"If we ever do again?" Probably not the part Trey should be focusing on, but his brain wasn't obedient at the best of times. "You think we might?"

"I don't know—sure, maybe."

"That's why you want me to stay?"

Seb shook his head almost violently. "No, that's about the only reason I *don't* want you to stay. I mean, it'd be a lot easier to have a quick fuck now and then if you weren't living right in my apartment."

"You lost me. What could be easier than an in-home fucktoy?"

"That right there!" Seb pulled his spoon out of the pot of oatmeal and pointed it in Trey's direction. "That's what makes it not easy. Worrying about all that shit. Like, were you just being sarcastic when you called yourself a fucktoy? Or were you covering up some deep-seated insecurity? Did I hurt your feelings, or insult you somehow, or are you being totally chill and fine and if I react then *I'm* the one who's taking shit too seriously and doesn't have the right perspective on it all?" He returned the spoon to the pot just before a glob of almost-cooked oatmeal fell off. "I don't have to worry about any of that if I just call up a stranger. Waiting twenty minutes for a guy to show up is *nothing* compared to the anxiety of trying to deal with someone I actually—I mean, not *care about* like in a romantic sense. But *care about* like it matters what you think and the world will get more complicated if you're hurt or sad or pissed off or whatever."

"And if I'm living here, you have to care about that."

"It's a potential complication, yeah." Seb jerked his chin toward one of the cupboards. "Get us bowls. There's milk and brown sugar in the fridge."

"Sugar goes in the fridge?"

"It's easy to find in there. Are the strawberries all rotten yet? If they're any good, pull them out too and slice them up."

Yeah, Seb didn't have any trouble making his wishes clear under normal circumstances, that was for sure. So Trey *could* stop worrying so much. "It's like we each have half a brain," he mused.

"What?"

"Not half a brain, but... like, you don't like deciding stuff when you're fucking, but you're pretty bossy all the rest of the time. And I'm kind of the opposite. I mean, I'm not too smart. It's generally best if other people decide stuff for me, mostly. If it's up to me, I just get in fights all the time. So, you know... You can boss me around most of the time, and when—I mean, *if*—we're fucking, I can boss you around."

"I can't actually say I've noticed you being all that open to taking my suggestions in the past."

"You had to earn it." Trey grinned. It felt good, like it made his whole face, and then even his brain, relax. And once that happened—once he stopped trying so hard to *think*—it was all clear to him. "Is your office expecting you at a certain time?"

"No," Seb said, his expression cautious, as if he'd noticed Trey's change in mood. "I set my own schedule. Why?"

"Turn off the stove," Trey said.

It was a simple order, but an order nonetheless. And that meant Seb wouldn't follow it, not if they were still having a normal conversation. He'd only do what Trey said if he was agreeing to—

He reached for the dial at the side of the stove, then shifted the pot off the burner for good measure.

Trey nodded. "Good." He felt his stomach muscles clench in anticipation, felt himself hardening. "Now, on your knees."

And Seb knelt.

"You're right," Trey mused as he took the two steps to bring himself next to Trey. "This is complicated. But you're remembering that you can say *no* at any time, and I'll stop. Just like if you tell me what to do in regular life and I don't want to, I can tell *you* no. Right?"

Seb nodded wordlessly and one hand drifted to the growing bulge in his sleep pants.

"Yeah, good. Touch yourself. You're going to suck me and jerk yourself off, and then we're going to have breakfast. After that, you can decide what we're going to do about the office and all the rest of it. Clear?"

Not even a nod this time, just Seb obediently—eagerly— reaching for Trey's fly.

Well, damn. Trey shifted so he could lean against the counter and let his eyes drift shut for a moment, then dragged them open again so he could look down and enjoy the view. He didn't think they'd solved anything, not really. But at least for the next few minutes, he didn't care, and that had to count for something.

Kate Sherwood

Chapter Ten

IT WASN'T HOW THINGS WERE supposed to happen. Seb wasn't supposed to give blowjobs to his one night stands the next morning; he wasn't supposed to eat breakfast with them afterwards; he wasn't supposed to drive them to his damn office; and he absolutely wasn't supposed to do all this and somehow be just fine with it.

It was strange how un-strange it all felt. When they got to the office, he told Trey to come up with him and Trey did as he was told and it seemed *normal*. A scowling thug trailing along behind Seb made several of the office staff do literal double-takes, but that was their issue, not Seb's. He found Gary in his office and updated him on the situation while Trey watched them both through half-closed eyes as if too disinterested to even pay attention, and the attitude wasn't annoying. It was too clearly rooted in defensiveness and insecurity, and if Seb was angry at anyone it was at the people who'd made Trey feel that way in the first place. As if he had nothing to contribute.

He'd been one of those people only days earlier, of course, but that wasn't something he needed to dwell on.

They made it back to Tristan's apartment in time for a meeting that essentially formalized the arrangements they'd already come up with—the buddy system, everyone keeping their phones charged and ready, and an added plan to make sure that anyone travelling after dark was either in a group or a car.

"We can't do this forever," Trey said. He didn't sound argumentative, just concerned.

"This is how girls have to do it all the time," Becky replied. "Like, there is literally nothing new about this for me, except that it might be easier for me to talk people into giving me rides home from work."

Trey scowled at her. "That sucks, but—I mean, it shouldn't be that way for you, and it shouldn't be this way for us. We should be able to walk around our own neighborhood without worrying about some assholes causing trouble."

Becky shrugged. "Yeah, that'd be nice. You let me know when you've got that problem solved, okay?"

Trey turned to Seb. "You're just going to accept this? You've got your safe life with your school and your family and the rest of it, and you're just—this is—it's how it's going to be?"

"I agree that it's not a good situation," Seb said. He honestly wasn't sure what Trey was looking for. "But I think it's better for us to take precautions than for one of us to get hurt."

"It'd be better for us to make them scared to mess with us," Trey said.

Oh. They were back to that. "We're still working on figuring out who 'they' even are."

"I should have gotten the license plate yesterday. That was our one chance to actually learn something, and I just—fuck, that cop who acted like I was stupid because I hadn't looked for it? He was right. I'm an idiot."

"Nah," Shane said. As far as Seb had seen, Trey and Shane had a fairly adversarial relationship, but Shane didn't seem reluctant to speak up in Trey's defense now. Maybe because he was defending Trey against himself? "I know how that is. You get that burst of adrenaline and all you're thinking about is how to fight and who could get you from which side—you're not in any condition to worry about remembering some stupid letters and numbers."

"Would have been nice if I had," Trey muttered, but he seemed mollified by Shane's words.

It was a family. Seb had thought it before, but watching Shane and Trey made it so much clearer. They might fight amongst themselves, but when it came down to it, they were all on the same side.

"We'll get back to work on the corporate records," Seb said. "I got some new ideas from Gary this morning, new places to look for information. Tracking down some hired thugs won't be nearly as useful as figuring out who's doing the hiring. That should be our priority, I think."

"Good," Becky said, standing up. "So—back to the Jungle for me and Trey? If the assholes didn't like us being up there, then that means we should keep doing it, right?"

"I'll come, too," Shane said. "Two people might be enough for most parts of town, but if we're going somewhere rough we should have more."

Trey looked like he was going to argue, but then Shane said, "And I'm not much use with all this reading," and Trey quietened down.

So the two of them stalked out together, Shane tall and lean, Trey shorter and thicker, both of them prowling like territorial cats. And Becky between them, looking delicate by comparison, clutching a bundle of flyers. They were a strange team, but a team nonetheless.

And Seb had his own compatriots, scattered around the apartment with laptops and tablets and pads of paper. Less dramatic, but still doing important work.

This wasn't what he'd expected when he'd signed up for the job, but he was part of it now, and he had no plans to back out.

~*~*~*~

SHANE WAS ABOUT AS ANNOYING as usual that day as they worked their way through the Jungle, but Trey found it surprisingly easy to ignore him. To ignore almost everything, really, with most of his mental energy focused in a completely different direction.

What was going to happen that night? Assuming he went back to Seb's, would they pick up where they'd left off that morning? Or would Seb have decided it was time to move on? Jesus, what if he invited someone else over? Trey could probably have handled it if that had happened the night before, but after the morning? After the thrill of giving Seb an order, of watching him obey without any signs of resistance or even thought—Seb was Trey's now.

Stupid to even pretend that was something that might be true, but damn it, Trey couldn't be expected to just sit in his room and— oh, god, not just *know* what was going on outside his door, but actually *hear* it. Hear Seb making those breathy little whimpering sounds for someone else, hear him groan and gasp like he had with Trey—

Trey kicked an empty beer can that had been resting by the side of the path they were walking on, and watched as it skittered over some rocks and then down a rough slope. Was there something else he could throw over the edge? Something that would smash into a million jagged pieces?

But there was nothing in sight, and Shane and Becky were looking at him as if wondering what his problem was, so he forced his face back into its neutral scowl.

"You good?" Becky asked.

If it had just been her, he might have told the truth. But Shane was—Shane. An ally, but not really a friend. So Trey growled, "I'm fine. What's next?" and they got back to work.

They dropped Becky off at work mid-afternoon, and on the way back to Tristan's Trey pointed out the overpass where the assholes had found him the day before.

"I wish they'd try something today," he said. "Three of them against you and me?"

Shane just nodded. Yeah, not a friend, but definitely an ally.

By the time they made it back to Tristan's the others were packing up, and Trey felt awkward. Just standing there, waiting for Seb, but what if Seb had changed his mind about having a house guest? What if he'd come to his damn senses?

Well, fuck it, Trey's stuff was still at the apartment, so he was heading over there, one way or another. "We going?" he demanded.

Seb raised an eyebrow. "Are you in a rush?"

"Is there a reason we're hanging around?"

The eyebrow lowered, and then the other joined it in a frown. "Chill out, okay?"

And there was a frozen moment when it seemed like Seb might be about to go a little further. Like he might turn his request into an order. And if he did, what then?

Everyone else was already watching them, trying to figure out what was going on. If Seb gave an order, would Trey actually follow it? If he did, what would it mean? What would it mean if he didn't? Jesus, this was too much, too fast, too strange—

But Seb didn't push it. "I want to wrap a few things up. About five minutes. That work for you?"

"Fine," Trey grunted. He turned, just a little too quickly, and made his way over to the window. It was easier there, to keep his back turned to the others, to have his attention outside while his body was inside, to balance himself halfway between two worlds without committing to either one. That was a good place to be.

So he stayed there until Seb was ready to leave, then followed him out the door and down the stairs.

"I'm going to my parents' place for dinner tonight," Seb said as they settled into his SUV. "I should be safe over there, right? And you'll stay in?"

Shit. Of course Seb wasn't going to be home all the time—he had a life, a family to visit. But for all Seb's weird talk, Trey didn't really belong in his apartment. He shouldn't be there on his own.

"I could go out, too," he tried. "I could wait—I don't know where, somewhere—until you came back, and you could let me in. Or—okay, your parking garage is secure, and your apartment is too nice for them to mess with, I'm sure, so you don't actually need me there. This whole thing is—"

Oh. Shit again. *You don't actually need me there.* Of course Seb didn't. It had taken Trey far too long to realize what was going on. "This whole thing is for me, not you. You don't need me there at all. You're just—"

103

If the car hadn't been moving, Trey would have opened the door and climbed out. His cheeks were heating, his muscles trembling. Too many emotions, too many ideas spinning around, making him almost dizzy. He needed to find somewhere quiet, somewhere *alone*, and just let himself calm down.

"No," Seb started, but he stopped talking when Trey raised a hand.

Trey had been pathetic to let himself be fooled for so long; he'd been *weak*, that was what he'd been. He'd wanted—well, nevermind what he'd wanted. He'd let himself think he was doing something useful, fooled himself into thinking he was contributing.

From the turmoil and confusion in his chest, he found his salvation: anger. Warm and familiar, and always there, waiting. "Jesus, you wanted a fuck that bad? You wanted a fucking house boy? Someone you could—" He felt sick, remembering the way he'd let himself be bossed around that morning. Going to the office like Seb had told him to, following him around like a damn puppy. He'd given up his pride, his control, because—fuck it, he had no idea why he'd done that. But he sure as hell wouldn't do it again.

They were at a stoplight, and Trey pushed his door open. "You're fine. You're safe. And I've got shit to do." He lurched out into the stopped traffic and slammed the car door. Already he was feeling stupid for making a fuss, and that just made him even angrier. At himself, at the world, at Seb—it didn't matter. He was mad at *everything*. Everyone.

The light turned green as he was making his way to the sidewalk and he assumed Seb drove off with the traffic; Trey didn't turn around to see. He just walked, and when people saw him coming and got out of his way, it felt good.

Yeah, they should be scared of him. He might not be smart enough to see when people were manipulating him, he might not be useful, but at least he was big, and scary. And if anyone didn't believe it, he'd be happy to prove it to them.

~*~*~*~

SEB CIRCLED THE BLOCK. What the hell was going on? What was he supposed to be doing, here?

His dad used to tell him to picture his life like a movie, himself as a character. And then, if there was a decision to be made, he could ask himself what a hero would do in that situation, and what a villain would do. And he should do the thing that the hero would do.

But how the hell would a hero react to this? A guy he barely knew got pissed at something he didn't really understand... so, what was the heroic response?

He'd completely lost track of Trey, so he pulled into a loading zone and dug out his phone. He didn't think an actual call was a good idea—whatever the hell Trey was pissed about, he definitely hadn't been ready for a logical conversation about it all. So Seb texted instead.

Your stuff is still at my place. Was that a cop-out? Probably. Seb kept typing. *You should stay there tonight. Longer if you want to. Talk to Tristan, or give me a call.* He hit send.

It wasn't enough, but what the hell else was he supposed to say? *Sorry you're homeless and I'm trying to help you out.* That wouldn't go over too well. *Sorry I made you feel like I was using you.* Shit, that might be justified.

Had Seb been using Trey?

They'd used each other, hadn't they?

But they'd had sex the way Seb wanted—sure, Trey had gotten off, and he'd seemed fairly into it, but just because he'd admitted that he'd gotten turned on by a couple stories Tristan had told, it didn't mean he was into—whatever the hell Seb was going to call it. Being an unofficial Dom, maybe. None of the rules, none of the theater, but only because that setup was what *Seb* wanted.

He pulled his phone back out of his pocket. *I have to go to my parents' for dinner.* And this wasn't going to be the sort of dilemma they'd be able to offer him a lot of guidance on, not unless he made it so vague and hypothetical as to be completely meaningless. *But I'd really like to see you later. Not for sex, just to talk. If you tell me where to pick you up, maybe around nine or ten, I'll come get you.* He hit send.

He read back over the texts and tried not to cringe at the thought of Trey showing them to anybody. They seemed too weak, too—too intimate. As if Seb actually *cared* whether Trey texted him. Which of course he didn't. He'd tried to help out, that was all.

He was a decent human being who didn't like to see others at risk or uncomfortable. If this was a movie, Seb was the hero for inviting Trey to stay with him.

And then making him fuck you just how you like it.

No, there'd been no *making*, surely. Except—

Damn it. Seb had taken one course on the Philosophy of Feminism and one on Social Justice and they'd combined to twist his brain up to the point he could barely function. Had there been a power imbalance? They'd been in Seb's territory, Seb clearly had more wealth than Trey, more education, more social currency— shit. More power.

Jesus, had he fucked up that badly? All his talk about wanting things to be real, to not mess around with the formal BDSM stuff… had he made it *too* real, but with the power play in the opposite direction of what he'd wanted?

I'm sorry if I did something you didn't want he typed. And then he slowly deleted the message. Was this—had it been *criminal*? Had it been that bad? Jesus, what had he done?

I'm sorry, he typed, and this time he sent the message.

He drove straight to his parents after that. It was just about the last place on the planet that he wanted to be—his mom and dad, both so wholesome and good, his sister and Talbot, confident and banal and accepting.

And Seb, squatting among them like a rat in a room full of bunny rabbits. Whatever he'd done—god, he needed to figure out what he'd done, needed to classify it, needed to get rid of the tight, horrible churning in his belly—they could never understand.

They'd support him. That was the worst part. They always had: through all the mistakes he'd made growing up, all the bad decisions and carelessness, they'd stood by him. They hadn't accepted his behaviour, and they certainly wouldn't now, not if he'd—god, what had he done, exactly—if he'd *hurt* Trey, somehow. Seb's family wouldn't tolerate that, but they'd still support Seb, as a person.

He pushed away from the dinner table far too abruptly. "I'm not feeling well," he told their concerned faces. "I need to go."

"You should stay here," his mother said. Of course she did. "You know your room's ready for you. Go upstairs and lie down for a while." She smiled gently, patiently, as if Seb was a little boy. "Try going to the bathroom. I'll come up and check on you in a bit."

She probably wanted to rub his tummy like she had when he was small and innocent. But he wasn't either of those things anymore. "No, I'm fine. I mean, I'm not fine, but I'll be fine at home."

"Your mom's a *doctor*," his father said calmly. "Why not take advantage of that?"

"I don't need a doctor. Just—okay, sure, when I get home I'll try going to the bathroom." Jesus, this was his life. "Sorry."

"Do you want us to drive you?" Allison asked, going into full older sister mode. "You could lie down for a few minutes while we have dessert, and then—"

But Allison was easier to ignore than his parents. "I'm fine." Seb forced a smile. "Sorry for the fuss. Gotta go."

"Call me when you get home," his mother called after him as he retreated. "And if you feel unwell on the drive, for god's sake pull over and one of us will come and get you."

Come get him and bring him back to safety and protection he wasn't sure he deserved.

As soon as he was out the door he pulled out his phone. *I'm kind of freaking out*, he typed. Too honest, but he was beyond caring. *What's going on? Can you please give me a call, or tell me where to come meet you?*

He waited in the driveway, hoping for a response, until he realized at least one member of his family was almost certainly spying on him from the house. He forced himself to drive at a reasonable speed for a few blocks, then swerved to the curb and typed *Fuck, Trey, could you PLEASE text back?*

But was Trey's phone even charged? Did he have minutes, and if he didn't, was he still able to get texts? Damn it, the son-of-a-bitch needed a better phone plan, one Seb could understand.

If you text me back, I'll get you a new phone plan, he typed, but then had enough sense to delete the message unsent.

He drove the rest of the way home, his mind racing from one possible action to another, but couldn't come up with anything that would make things better, short of talking to Trey and figuring out exactly what was actually wrong.

A few turns around the neighborhood turned up nothing, so Seb parked and stomped up the stairs to his apartment. At the top of the stairwell he paused, and suddenly knew what he'd see when he opened the door. Trey would be sitting by Seb's apartment door, leaning against the wall, legs stretched out like he didn't care whether he blocked the hallway or not. He'd be grumpy, maybe, but not truly angry anymore, and he'd let Seb herd him inside and they'd eat something and have a few beers and talk things through, and when they were done taking—well, Seb had no idea what they'd do then.

And it didn't matter anyway, because when he pulled the door open, the hallway was empty.

He wanted to turn back around and do some more searching, but of course it was pointless. Seattle was too big, Trey too clearly uninterested in being found. So Seb went back inside, made his duty call to his mother, lied and said he was feeling better already, then flopped onto his sofa and stared at his phone.

He had to do it.

He dialled and heard Tristan's cheerful, "Hey, Seb."

"Hi. Uh, weird question, but is Trey over there with you?"

"Trey? He's supposed to be with you."

Yes, damn it, he *was* supposed to be with Seb. But he wasn't, and Seb needed to be honest about it. "He left. Didn't even make it back to the apartment before he got mad about—I'm not sure, but I

110

think it was my fault—and he got out of the car and I haven't seen him since. He won't answer my texts."

Tristan was silent for a moment, then said, "One time Trey punched Micah for not eating his pizza crusts. Just on the shoulder, not the face, and Micah was too stoned to really care, but—it left a pretty big bruise. Trey's just—he's a pretty angry person. Doesn't have to be anything you did or didn't do."

It was certainly tempting to accept that excuse. But Seb wasn't sure he could. "I guess I can try to sort that out when we find him. For now, though, his stuff's all here, and he's not supposed to be out there alone, right? I mean, if he's planning to sleep outdoors he'll probably go back to your neighborhood? Does that make sense? He wouldn't want to mess with the cops and the security guards and whatever around here."

"And if he comes back here there's a better chance of him running into the assholes who want to mess him up," Tristan said. "Shit. Okay, uh—I'll try to get in touch with him and get him to come over here. Maybe he's not mad at me."

Yeah, maybe you didn't pressure him into having sex. "Okay, yeah. I'll—I don't know, I guess I'll stick around here in case he shows up?" It seemed useless, but Seb wasn't sure what else he could do.

"Okay. And look, man—he's not a little kid. He can take care of himself—I mean, have you *seen* him? No-one's going to mess with him. He'll be fine."

"No ONE's going to mess with him. But there were three guys yesterday. And it sounds like they've got their own network of informants set up, since they knew what Trey and Becky'd been doing in the Jungle. If one of their spies sees Trey, alone...."

"I'll call him," Tristan promised. "It'll be fine."

It helped a little, but not enough. Seb still found himself pacing restlessly around the apartment, peering out the windows to the street below as if expecting to see Trey down there under one of the streetlights. He checked the hallway a few more times, too, but Trey wasn't there.

Of course he wasn't. He was angry. Probably for good reason. He wasn't going to show up at the apartment of the person he was angry with.

The next time Seb picked up his phone he forced himself to dial the number instead of sending a text. The texts had been cowardly, under the circumstances. He'd been trying to shield himself from dealing with Trey head-on, but direct communication was exactly what was needed. It's what should have happened— should have happened better—right from the start.

The phone rang three times, and then there was an answer. Trey's voice, but quieter than Seb had been expecting. "Seb? Fuck. Can you call Tristan? Tell him—shit. Get Shane."

There were muffled voices in the background, and sounds of movement. "Trey? What's going on?"

"Tell them I'm at the park. By the walkway." Trey sounded— scared? No, but excited, and not in a completely pleasant way.

112

"Okay, but—"

The other voices were louder now, and there was a muffled clatter—the phone being dropped—and then yelling. Trey's voice, and definitely others—

"Trey!" Seb was on his feet, moving, running, but going where? Whatever was going on was far away, and happening fast, and there was nothing Seb could do about it.

"Trey!" he yelled again, and now he was out in the hallway, bashing his fist into his neighbor's door, again and again. Come on, neighbor! Seb couldn't remember their names, didn't care about their damn names, he just needed—

The door opened and he yelled "I need your phone! Call the cops! My friend's in trouble, and I don't want to hang up on him—" Not that the sounds coming over the phone were in any way intelligible, but the call was the only connection Trey had, and Seb couldn't stand the thought of hanging up on him and leaving him all alone.

"Two phones," he demanded. Two neighbors, and surely each had a phone. "One of you call the cops. The other—" He forced himself to pull his phone away from his ear and quickly scrolled through his contacts without hanging up on the call. "This number," he told the woman who appeared in the doorway next to her husband, phone in hand. "Call this number, ask for Tristan, tell him that Trey's in trouble at the park, near the walkway. We need to know what park that is, where it is, so we can send the police there."

Her eyes were wide but she nodded and tapped the number into the phone with steady fingers.

Seb lifted his cell back to his ear and listened desperately. "Trey! Hey, Trey, you there?"

There was no answer for far too long, although there were still sounds—rustling, some distant shouts—nothing that offered any kind of reassurance.

Then a sharper kind of static, and a voice. Male, out of breath—not Trey. "He was warned," the man said, and then the line went dead.

Chapter Eleven

IT HAD ALL UNFOLDED LIKE a chaotic dream after that. A nightmare, really. Coordinating with Tristan and the police, racing down to Seb's own car, getting half-way to the park before getting Tristan's call that Trey had been found, and was on the way to the hospital in an ambulance.

"Is he okay?" Seb had demanded. Stupid question, of course—people who were okay didn't get taken to the hospital.

But Tristan didn't point that out. "He—I don't know. He was unconscious. We're following them in a cab. If you want to meet us—"

Of course Seb wanted to meet them.

But by the time he made it to the hospital there was already a crowd of familiar faces in the waiting room, and most of them didn't seem too pleased to see him.

"I thought he was supposed to be with you," Shane said, his voice accusing. Damn, he seemed bigger than usual. Bigger, and meaner.

115

"I told you already," Tristan broke in. "Seb called me about that; he can't be expected to control Trey when none of the rest of us can."

"How is he?" Seb asked. He kept his attention on Tristan, who seemed the least hostile.

"We're waiting to hear. Simon got hold of the paramedics and they said he came to in the ambulance, but that he was kinda—" Tristan looked uncomfortable. "Kinda messed up. They had to strap him down."

"But he's alive." It felt strange to say the words, to admit to the fear. Still, now that he'd said it, he wanted to spend a bit of time reassuring himself about it. "They didn't kill him."

"Not this time," Jake said bleakly.

Shit. This was probably the first time Jake had been in a hospital since his brother died. He didn't need this reminder, this echo of the tragedy. But he was there all the same, giving what support he could. And hopefully taking some as well.

"It's bullshit," Shane said, his voice too loud for a public space. "Trey was right—we can't just sit back and let them pick us off one by one. We need to hit back. The cops were asking questions like they thought Trey asked for this, like it was a fight, not a beating. They're not going to be any use. We need to figure out who did this." He turned to Seb. "That's *your* fucking job, isn't it? You're supposed to be figuring out who these bastards are so we can go after them."

"He's only had a few days," Tristan said. "Come on, guys, we need to stay calm. If we can just focus on Trey right now—"

"Focus on what?" Shane growled, with a glare in the general direction of the nurses' station. "They aren't telling us shit. We're not his fucking *family*, so we don't get to know anything."

Well, that, at least, Seb could help with.

He paused for half a second as he wondered how his mom would react to the call, then hit the speed dial number anyway.

"Baby?" she answered, her voice groggy from sleep. "Are you feeling worse?"

He turned and took a few steps away from the crowd. "No, I'm okay. But—I'm sorry I woke you up. But can you help me out with something? A friend—a guy I work with—he got mugged or something tonight. I don't know all the details. But he's at your hospital, and he hasn't got any family or anything, but his friends are all here and they want to know how he is. He's unconscious or incoherent or something—we can't even figure that much out, but he's not in a state to give consent. So the staff isn't giving us any information—"

"Good," his mother said firmly. "They're following the rules. Patient confidentiality is a serious matter, Sebastian."

"Yeah, I know, but—look, I've spent enough time with these people to know that they're essentially his family. And they're really worried about him." *And I need to be able to contribute* something *to this damn mess, Mom. Come on, help me out.*

Seb managed to keep himself from speaking the words, but possibly maternal telepathy came into play, because after a moment's thought his mom said, "You're sure he has no family?"

"None that he's in touch with."

Another pause, and then his mother said, "The phrase you'll want to use is 'support person'. If you tell whoever is in charge that you—or whoever else—are the patient's support person, they'll share necessary information with you."

"Yeah? That easy?"

"I'll make sure it is—unless you give them some reason to not believe you."

"Cool. And how do I find out who's in charge?"

She sighed. Yeah, okay, he should be able to handle something like this on his own, but—she was his mom. She'd be happy he'd come to her for help, once she got past being crabby about the interrupted sleep.

"I'll call Bill Ondaatje. You know Bill. He's working nights this week; he'll come find you. What's your friend's name?"

"Trey—" And for a horrible moment, Seb's mind blanked. What the hell was Trey's last name? He'd just told his mom they were friends, he was willing to sign on as the guy's "support person", whatever that meant, but he didn't know his last name? No, he'd seen it, he was sure of it. Back in the beginning, written on the attendance sheet for that first general meeting—"Fiso," he said, trying to keep the triumph out of his voice. "Trey Fiso."

"Okay. Trey Fiso. I'll call Bill—you sit tight."

She hung up, and only a few minutes later a harried looking doctor strode into the waiting room, a big smile on his face when he saw Seb. Impossible to be sure how much of the enthusiasm was genuine and how much was related to kissing up to the son of the Chief of Staff.

"Seb, good to see you." Dr. Ondaatje's handshake was firm. "Your mother said you were hoping for a bit of personalized attention?"

And Seb was suddenly aware of how this would look to the others. These weren't his school friends; they weren't going to be impressed by his ability to pull strings, they were going to be resentful and think he was showing off. Hell, maybe his school friends felt the same way, but they put up with him in order to earn their right to show off their own connections when their turns came. "Just basic information," Seb said quickly. "Trey Fiso is a friend of—well, of ours." *Don't start thinking about it, don't let yourself wonder if Trey would want you claiming that title.* "I'm his support person, if that matters. He's—" God, Seb needed to stop talking, but still he came out with the absurdity of "We live together," before managing to shut up.

Dr. Ondaatje's smile was a little more fixed than it had been earlier, but there were no other signs of surprise. "Okay," he said. "Trey is currently in stable but serious condition. We're monitoring his head injury very closely—there's been significant swelling, which can lead to permanent damage if it isn't controlled. We've given him some medication to aid his healing, but it's made him temporarily non-responsive, so we can't conduct a full assessment of any cognitive issues. There are several broken bones—his right hand will require the attention of an orthopedic specialist, and there are fractures to—" Dr. Ondaatje broke off. "This may be more detail than you need. For now—we're most concerned with the head trauma. We're monitoring that, and keeping an eye on the internal bleeding caused by damage to his torso. The broken bones will be dealt with down the line."

"So—he'll be okay. He's messed up now, but he'll be okay?"

Dr. Ondaatje smiled. "We hope so. If we can keep the cranial swelling under control, and if there hasn't been damage done that we haven't yet observed, he should be able to make a full recovery." His expression grew more serious. "But it will not be a simple process. And he'll need help. As his support person—well, he'll need you. And—we don't have any information on his insurance company…."

"Yeah," Seb said quickly. "Insurance. I'll look into that, see what I can find."

"And if he doesn't have insurance, get your mother involved as soon as possible. There are things we can do, but they take time. She can help speed the process up."

"Okay, yeah—thanks. Uh, when can we see him?"

"He's unconscious now—we're planning to keep him that way for at least twelve hours. So there's not actually any point in visitors. It would make more sense to rest up and be ready to be with him when he's actually aware of your presence."

It made sense, intellectually, but it just didn't feel right. "You're sure he's not, like, *aware* of his surroundings? I know, he's unconscious, but you hear stories about people still knowing what's going on...."

"He's *deeply* unconscious. He won't know if you're there." The doctor looked around as if aware for the first time of the audience hovering just out of hearing range. "And he won't be ready for a crowd for some time. We'd say family only under most circumstances, but if his family isn't involved, we'd work with you—and with him, once he's able—to figure out a list of people who can see him *one at a time*. Honestly, by the time he's ready to deal with this many people all at once we'll be ready to discharge him, so—work out a schedule of some sort. It's good to see he has support, but you'll need to keep it low-key. Understood?"

Seb nodded. He understood the doctor all too well; what he couldn't quite understand was how he'd gotten himself into this situation. He was the support person? He didn't know exactly what that meant, but it seemed to involve being in charge, somehow. Seb had known Trey for a few days, total. Sure, they'd fucked, but so had Trey and Becky, and maybe Trey and other members of the group, too. Tristan was the den mother, the nurturer, the one who should be sitting by Trey's bedside.

Seb closed his eyes for a long moment, opened them to see Dr. Ondaatje waiting patiently, then pulled himself together enough to say a few polite words of thanks before the doctor went back to his work. Then Seb turned to the others.

"Could you hear most of that?"

"Some. But give it to us again, okay?"

"Did you tell him Trey was *living with you?*" Shane interjected. "What the fuck? You know that sounded like—like you're *living together.* Not like Trey spent the night in your spare bedroom."

"Yeah, I kinda panicked. I didn't know how much I had to say to get the information."

Shane's glower held for another couple seconds before it turned into a grin. "Man. Talk about an odd couple. You and Trey—and that guy actually believed it?"

"No," Seb started, but Shane held up a hand to interrupt.

"Tell us what the doctor said," he ordered.

Okay, that first, and clarifications later. So Seb summarized what he'd been told, including the instructions to rest up in preparation for later visits. "And, look," he said. He didn't want to say it, but someone had to. "On the phone—the guy said they'd already given a warning. This was—it was an escalation, because we didn't listen last time. I think—I'm not saying we should give up. But I think we need to take a hard look at things and figure out how much of a risk we're willing to take."

He looked around at the others' faces. "We can keep working on it. Maybe more through the Seattle Communities Team, rather than front-line stuff."

"So they win?" Shane demanded. He looked almost as aggressive as Trey at his worst, and Seb wasn't sorry to see Noah's hand reaching out to soothe, or possibly to restrain.

"They want us to stop, so we stop?" Jake's objection wasn't as loud as Shane's, but there was an intensity that made everyone else fall silent. "They killed my brother. They beat the shit out of Trey. So we back off?"

"We don't play *their* game," Seb tried. "They know who we are, so it's easy for them to watch us and wait for one of us to make a mistake. We don't know who they are, so we can't do the same. We need to play *our* game instead."

"And what *is* our game?" Tristan this time, calm and gentle, but still strong.

It felt like an important moment, like a test. Not one set by the people in front of him, but by the universe. Could Seb channel their energy? Could he protect them from their own recklessness? Did he actually have something to contribute to all this or was he just another college kid padding his resume?

"I'm not sure," he admitted. "But I think—we should meet, and talk it over and decide what strategy we want to take. But I wonder if the next step is—me."

"You?" Simon asked.

"I'm a rich white kid," Seb told them. "I'm good looking— you know you've all been admiring me, so don't even try to pretend I'm not—and I'm well-spoken. I'm non-threatening. If I go to the media and explain what happened—what I *heard* happening, and what the asshole—I won't use that word, we'll have to come up with a better one that's less aggressive, more responsible—but if I tell the world what the asshole said to me, it—I wish it wasn't true, guys, but coming from me—"

Tristan waved a hand as if dismissing Seb's attempts to be sensitive. "Yeah, we get it. You'd be good. People would listen to you, and they'd believe you. But—so what? Does it really matter if they do?"

"Uh, yeah." Seb squinted at Tristan, trying to figure out if there was a hidden question he wasn't seeing. "That's our main approach, right? To get public opinion on our side?"

"Our side, or your side?" Tristan asked. "If people believe you, does that mean they're going to want to help a bunch of—" He looked around at his friends, then shrugged as he turned back to Seb. "—a bunch of *us*? Or the other people in the neighborhood, all the ones who *aren't* good looking, rich white kids?"

"If I do it right they will."

That was met with silence, which was almost certainly more than Seb deserved. He'd known these people for only a few days, and he was asking them to trust him with something like this. It was too much. Far too much, especially when a friend was in trouble.

"I don't think we need to decide anything right now," he said quickly. "I just wanted to say that even if we ease off on the stuff the assholes want us to stop doing, it wouldn't mean we'd given up altogether. We'd just be redirecting our efforts."

"And redirecting their attention," Simon said slowly. "You think you're safe? You think just being a rich, white, pretty boy is enough to keep them from messing with you?"

"I think being the face of the resistance would be enough to keep them from messing with me," Seb said firmly. He was pretty sure he was right. He thought of Trey, lying in a hospital bed, drugged into unconsciousness for his own good, his own healing, and all of it because Seb had screwed up and driven Trey away from safety. Yeah, hopefully Seb was right that he'd be safe, but even if he wasn't it was a chance he was willing to take. "If I focus the attention on *me*, they won't be able to mess with me without bringing even *more* attention to the issue, and attention is what they don't want."

"We *hope* it's what they don't want," Tristan said. Not arguing, just clarifying.

Seb shrugged his acquiescence. "Okay, yeah. Without knowing exactly who they are—we need to keep working on that—this is just an educated guess. But I think it makes sense."

"And in the fall when you go back to school?" Simon's voice was as level as Tristan's had been. Damn, the two of them were a good team.

"We need to talk all this over. But—yeah, I went into this thinking it'd be something long-term and I'd just be around for the startup stages. But I'm wondering if it isn't going to happen faster than we thought. If these guys are ramping up the pressure like they are? Either the foot soldiers are out of control, which seems like a good opportunity, or they're following orders to get things tidied up fast, which *also* seems like a good opportunity. Honestly, this could be taken care of before—"

"Before Trey's out of the hospital?" It was Becky, speaking for the first time, her swollen eyes and tear-stained face making it clear why she'd been quiet. "Before he's back on the street, getting hurt *again* because we've all decided to get worked up about who owns some stupid buildings none of us can even afford to live in *now*? I mean, why the hell is this our business?"

Seb froze. She was right. Completely right. How could he ask any of these people to risk what little they had in pursuit of something as nebulous and rarified as anti-gentrification? Why the hell *should* they care?

"Because of Austin," Micah said quietly. He was focused on Becky, but he glanced at Jake as if for confirmation, and clearly got the response he was looking for. "Because these fuckers *made* it our business when they started killing us, treating us like we were fucking rats that had to be exterminated to make the property more valuable."

"Because of Dodger, and Andy, and Raven and Jory and Jayden," Shane said. Dodger was the dog, but Seb had no idea who the other people were. The rest of the gang seemed to recognize the names, though. "It was a different asshole who messed with them, I know," Shane continued. "But it's the same fucking idea. Somebody wants something and isn't afraid to hurt us to get it, because he thinks we don't matter. Without money and families and all that crap, we're nothing. But fuck that. We're something. We matter."

"And because of Trey," Tristan added. He flashed his beautiful, genuine smile at Becky. "You think he's not going to want revenge for this? I mean, if we don't have it all figured out before he's better, he's going to—" He shook his head. "God only knows what he's going to do. But he's not going to walk away, and you know it."

"But *you* can," Seb said quickly. He was pretty sure he was speaking for Trey as he said it. "This needs to be everyone's own decision. No pressure, no sense of obligation. Everyone has to look at their own safety and decide how much of a risk they can take. Honestly—" He looked at the others for support, then turned his attention back to Becky. "I bet Trey would be thrilled if you dropped out. You know he worries about you."

She stared back at him. "You think I'm going to walk away when nobody else is?"

"Maybe somebody else will, too." Seb shrugged. "It doesn't mean you don't care, it just means—"

"It means they scared me," she said. "They got what they wanted by beating Trey up."

"Ignore them," Seb suggested. "Do what's right for you."

"What's right for me." There was something heartbreaking about the way she said the words, as if they reflected a mindset she'd never considered before. She frowned for a moment, and then her expression cleared. "Yeah, okay." She nodded and looked around at the group. "It's right for me to live in a world where bullies don't get what they want. Where people can't mess with Andy or Dodger or Jake's brother without something happening. Trey might not want me involved—" She grinned suddenly. "But he'll have to haul his ass out of bed before he can do anything about it. So for now, I'm in, and when he's better—well, you said this might all be taken care of by then, right?"

The attention all turned back to Seb, and he wanted to run away. He was a fraud. He had no business presenting himself as any sort of an expert. He'd finished three years of a bachelor's degree—that was all.

"It may be resolved quickly," Simon said, smooth as usual. Bailing Seb out, either accidentally or deliberately. "I agree that there seems to be more urgency coming from the other side than we'd expected, and I agree that there's potential to take advantage of that. But—" He shrugged. "No guarantees."

"We need to talk to Gary, and all the others, too. The shopkeepers, the other people involved in the movement." Seb waited for objections, but none came. "I can ask the Communities Team if we can use their space, if you want. It would be less—less of a target than meeting at Tristan's."

There was general consensus, and then an awkward pause. "Does everyone have a safe way to get home?" Seb asked. "Teams, and cab fare and whatever?"

"We're just going to leave him here alone?" Becky demanded, clearly ready to fight again.

"I was planning to stay," Seb said. "My mom works here, and there's a couch in her office where I can sleep until she comes to work tomorrow." He knew he should offer to let more of them crowd in with him, but there were going to be enough awkward questions from his mother already; he really didn't want to sign up for more.

"And they'll tell you if he wakes up?" Becky asked.

"Yeah. I'll give them my cell number."

"Okay," she said. "You take the first shift. Then when you have to go to the meeting tomorrow, I'll come here and be with him."

Seb was surprised by how wrong that felt. Because—oh, shit. Because it should be *him* sitting by Trey's bedside, should be *his* face that Trey saw first when he woke up.

Yeah, show him your face so he can get pissed off again and let himself get hurt because he can't stand to be around you. Brilliant plan, asshole.

"Sounds good," he managed. Because it did. It was a good plan. Totally fair, and best for Trey, and that was what mattered.

So Seb made his way to his mom's office and entered the code, then texted her so she'd know he was there. Then he kicked off his shoes and lay down on the couch.

Trey was unconscious somewhere in that same building. He was hurt bad enough that the doctors weren't promising anything about his recovery.

And he was there because Seb hadn't done his damn job. If Trey'd stayed with Seb, he would have been safe at home. Bored, sure, but safe. Instead...

Seb had screwed up. He still didn't know just how badly he'd misunderstood the situation, but it was crystal damn clear that he hadn't been careful enough. And Trey was the one suffering for it.

Seb wouldn't let himself wriggle away from that truth. He wouldn't make excuses or try to minimize things. He'd fucked up.

The sofa was too short for him to stretch out, but it wasn't physical discomfort that made it so difficult for him to get to sleep that night.

Chapter Twelve

THE SOUNDS CAME BACK FIRST. Distant and muddled, like trying to listen to a TV show in another room. With some of Seb's damn oatmeal in his ears.

Then there was a vague sensation of gravity, of things touching his body and making him way heavier than he usually was.

Then sight, and damn, was that ever a mistake. Everything too bright, too much, and Trey threw his arm up over his eyes to try to block it out, but his arm was tangled in something and so were his legs, and his other arm was tied down? He fought to sit up, but hands pushed on his shoulder, and someone yelled at him, this time not through oatmeal at all.

"Trey, calm down," Becky ordered. She sounded scared, and Trey needed to fix that. He needed to be standing up to fix it.

"Trey, you're fine," a different voice said. Older than Becky, female… no one he knew. "You're in the hospital, Trey. We're taking care of you. Your friends are with you. You're okay, and we're going to help you. Please relax, Trey."

131

The hospital? What?

But there was something in the way she spoke that made him believe her, and he let himself relax a little. He sagged into—yeah, okay, that was a mattress, and maybe it was a blanket that was tangling his legs up, and maybe his one arm, too, but there was something wrong with his other arm. He yanked, and whatever was holding him back didn't give.

"We have an IV in that arm," the older woman said calmly. "We have a soft restraint on it because you were agitated and we thought you might rip the IV out. If you're ready, I can take the restraint off. Can you show me that you understand what I'm saying?"

Show her? What was he supposed to do, interpretive dance?

He forced his eyes open instead, squinting against the brightness, and saw a white blur move to the side of the room and then lift her arm—and the light dimmed to something more tolerable.

"I'm okay," he tried, and it sounded like his mouth was full of the same damn oatmeal that had been blocking up his ears.

"Why does he sound like that?" Becky demanded, and for the first time it occurred to Trey that maybe *he* was what she was afraid of.

"The medication will take some time to wear off," the older woman said. Still calm, still confident. "We'll do more of an assessment later, but for now there's absolutely nothing to worry about."

"Arm," Trey said, trying to be helpful. The state of his speech wasn't his main concern right then.

And the older woman seemed better at interpreting his mumbling than Becky was, because there were cool, efficient hands at his wrist, and then he was free.

"Who?" he managed.

He managed to focus, at least for a moment, on the face that hovered over him. "I'm Dr. Emma Tanner. I'm the Chief of Staff here, but I'm also Sebastian's mother."

Seb's mom. Even here, Seb was in charge. *Especially* here, in this clean, white, far-too-bright place.

Trey should—he wasn't sure what he should do. Definitely not just lie there in the soft, warm hospital bed. But everything was so damn heavy. When he opened his eyes, it was too confusing, and still too bright. He needed to gather his strength. Just a little nap, and then he'd be ready to fight. Somebody. Whoever needed to be fought, he'd fight them. But he'd do it... later.

~*~*~*~

"HE WOKE UP?" SEB DEMANDED. "You were there?" His mother was the Chief of Staff at a major hospital; she didn't spend much time sitting by patients' bedsides. And they were now back in her office, where she *did* spend most of her time. "Did he—did he say anything?" *Did he accuse me of anything? Did he tell you that*

133

your son dragged him into his deviant world without consent?

"He was groggy. He has a neurology appointment first thing tomorrow morning, and we'll have a better picture of his situation then."

"Tomorrow morning?" It was late afternoon—according to his mom, Trey had woken for the first time hours ago, when Seb was at the damn meeting at Seattle Communities' headquarters. "Not now? What if there's—I don't know, something that we should be doing in the meantime?"

"Sebastian." His mother fixed him with her patented I'm Being Patient; You're Being Absurd stare. "Everyone knows you're my son, and everyone knows he's your friend. Do you honestly think anyone's going to cut corners on this?"

It should have been reassuring, and in a way, it was. Trey would get the best care possible, and that was a good thing.

But, damn it, he'd only get it because Seb's mommy had stepped in?

"This is what they were talking about this afternoon," he said. He was thinking out loud, but his mom might as well hear it straight from the source. "If you don't have money, or power or prestige or something... if you're just a regular person, without connections... the system doesn't work. If your brother gets killed by arsonists and you're just a landscaper, nothing happens. If there's nobody with influence involved, it just gets swept under the rug. Just one more statistic, one more dead junkie."

"That's not fair—"

"Exactly! It's not *fair*, mom. These are real people. Trey—he's a real person! If he hadn't run into me by chance, how would things be working for him? He's in a private room, for god's sake." He softened his tone. "I mean—thank you. For taking an interest in him, and making sure he's getting the best care. But there shouldn't *be* a best care, should there? It should just be *care*, for everybody, no matter who they are or who they know."

His mother was quiet for a moment. Just before his sense of guilt grew strong enough to overwhelm his sense of outrage, she said, "You're right. Of course. But the world isn't about what 'should' be. There are realities. *Financial* realities. Trey isn't going to be paying for any of this." She saw his expression and snorted. "Oh, please. Nobody bought your 'his insurance paperwork must be lost somewhere' nonsense. We know he hasn't got insurance, and it's pretty clear he hasn't got personal resources. And that's fine—I'll take care of it. I've already spoken to the social workers and there are programs in place to pay for at least *some* of this. And we can find space for the rest."

"Space," Seb echoed. Some discretionary fund, some stash of money tucked away in a forgotten budget line. A perk that could be accessed by those in the know. The sort of thing Seb had been benefiting from his whole life. And he was only noticing it now because it was going to help someone else instead of himself.

"It'll be taken care of," she said, but the words weren't as reassuring as she clearly meant them to be. "You can go see him if you'd like. But in the meantime—your father and I want some time with you. He's agreed to come by the hospital on his way home from the office, so why don't you go visit your friend and I'll have someone get a message to you when your dad gets here."

"Some time?" That was parent-speak for a big conversation about something they knew Seb didn't want to discuss. "Why? Did Trey say something?" Oh, god, what had he said? What had he told Seb's *mother*?

But she'd just suggested Seb go see Trey. Just called him Seb's friend. Surely that meant Trey had kept his mouth shut, at least temporarily. But then—

"We're concerned about this job," she said. "It seems like it's too much—too dangerous. We'd like to discuss some options with you, ways to make sure you don't get involved in something you shouldn't be."

It took him a moment to reorient himself in the conversation. "The job? It's—no, it's fine. Trey got hurt because he was alone, and he's one of the people who's been out in the community stirring things up. It's not something that's going to affect *me*."

"People have already *died*, Sebastian! Living in a secure building *helps*, I'm sure, but it's still a risk you don't need to be taking." Then she held up her hand in a gesture of authority he recognized far too well. "But your father wants to be part of this conversation too. We'll wait until he gets here before we discuss options."

"There are no options," he retorted.

"Go see your friend. And, Seb—really *see* him. I'm reasonably optimistic that we aren't going to find any permanent damage to his cognitive abilities—no brain damage—but look at what they *did* to him. They could have killed him—who knows, maybe they thought they had. These people you're facing are not playing by the rules you've grown up with. Look at your friend and understand what's at risk."

As if there was some chance Seb wouldn't see that. But his mother needed to realize it was *Trey* and the rest of them she should be worrying about, not Seb with his safe car, safe apartment—safe life.

"I'll go check on him," he agreed. No point having the fight separately with his mom and then having to repeat the whole thing when his dad arrived.

He checked his cell phone in the elevator and saw there was a message from Gary. He probably wanted to debrief after the big meeting, and Seb wasn't too sorry to have a distraction that would keep him from having to face Trey right away. The injuries weren't a concern, but he couldn't forget that Trey had only been in a position to *be* injured because of what Seb had done. The guilt from that was enough to make him pretty happy to get off the elevator at the cafeteria level and find a quiet corner to return Gary's call.

"Seb! Thanks for calling back. I wanted to speak to you after the meeting, but you disappeared pretty quickly."

"I wanted to come to the hospital to check in on Trey."

"Absolutely, absolutely—fair enough!" Gary sounded like a used-car salesman, all forced jocularity and excessive enthusiasm.

"What's going on?" Seb asked.

"Well, Seb—I've spoken to the executive panel, and we're all in complete agreement about this—and I want to stress that it's in no way a reflection on your performance, or on your judgment. More a reflection on ours, to be honest. We didn't understand the situation clearly enough going in, or we never would have assigned you to such a dangerous task."

"Dangerous? What? Gary, I'm fine. I'm not in danger. It's *Trey* who got hurt, and the rest of the people living in that neighborhood who are at risk. Not *me*." Jesus, why was everyone worrying about *him*?

"Trey and the others living in that neighborhood are a concern, of course, but, Seb—they're not our employees. Not our responsibility. You are. It's a problem—a legal problem, in terms of employment law and our duty of care, but also a potential PR nightmare. You know our funding model—governmental support, but also significant contributions from private donors. If it came out that we were sending our summer interns into dangerous situations? If, god forbid, something actually *happened* to you? It wouldn't just be a lawsuit issue, it would be a funding issue. So, I'm sorry, Seb, but the executive panel, with my full agreement, has decided to reassign you for the remainder of your internship."

It was impossible. Surreal, almost. Trey was lying in a hospital bed and the world was scrambling to make sure that *Seb* was okay?

"Reassign me to *what*?" It wasn't the most important question, not by a long shot, but hearing it answered would give Seb a bit of time to reorganize the rest of his thoughts.

"Oh, there are a variety of exciting projects you could choose from!" The used-car salesman was back. "We have a group working on community gardens—it seems like such a simple concept, but you'd be surprised by the amount of organization and coordination that goes into getting one set up. Or another team is doing a study on the distribution of daycare spaces in high-income vs. low-income neighborhoods. That's mostly research-based, but you can't deny that it's an important social justice issue! I think you could contribute a lot to that project!"

Seb forced himself to pull the phone away from his ear and take a deep breath, then release it. He sounded much calmer than he felt when he said, "I'd prefer to stay on the current project, thanks."

"I'm afraid that's not going to be an option," Gary said. Not a car salesman now—more like a parent telling the kids the goldfish had died. "But we'll find something else for you to be passionate about. Come in to the office tomorrow, first thing, and we'll talk."

"I'm going to argue in favor of no change," Seb said. No point being coy.

"We'll talk tomorrow," Gary said. "For now, check in on Trey—give him our best, okay?"

Seb muttered some vaguely appropriate reply, then hung up and stood there staring at his phone. His parents *and* Gary? The damn executive council of the organization? They all thought he was going to quit as soon as things got difficult?

They had another think coming. He wasn't going to give in on this, and he'd make that crystal clear to his parents that evening and the council the next day.

But in the meantime—he'd delayed as long as he could. He needed to go see Trey. Needed to face the consequences of his own carelessness and irresponsibility.

Once that was over, standing up to his parents and his bosses should be a piece of cake.

Chapter Thirteen

TREY WAS DOZING, JUST AS he'd been for most of the day, when he heard a new voice. The nurses, or Seb's mom, or whoever was in charge, had said he could only have one visitor at a time, and that had been fine, really. He didn't mind closing his eyes if it was just Becks or Tristan sitting beside the bed, but if the whole gang had been there he would have felt like a weakling for doing it.

But now, Becky was there, and she was talking to—

Trey eased his eyes open, just a slit, enough to see the new arrival.

Seb was standing at the foot of the bed, and he looked—nervous. What did he have to be nervous about?

Oh. Maybe he thought Trey was still mad at him.

Which was a good point. Maybe Trey *was* still mad at him.

Except Trey didn't have the energy for any of that shit, not right then. He'd go back to being mad later, when he felt better.

"Hey," he grunted, and let his eyes open a little more.

"Hi," Seb said. He shuffled his feet, glanced at Becky, then back to Trey. "You're okay, then? I mean, messed up, but—okay?"

"Your mom seems to think so," Trey said. Then he frowned. It hurt to frown. "I didn't mean that in a 'your momma' way. Just—she seems to think I'm okay."

Seb made a little laughing noise—not forced, but like he'd surprised himself by being amused. "Okay, good. Thanks for the clarification."

"We're not supposed to have two people in here at the same time," Becky said. She sounded annoyed, as if it was pretty clear to her which one of them should be leaving.

"Oh," Seb said, back to seeming unsure and nervous. "Okay. So—I can just go, I guess. But they're going to kick visitors out around eight—have you got a ride home?"

Becky looked at Trey as if expecting him to help her out, but what the hell was he supposed to do? "Jake said I could call him if I needed."

"I can drop you off," Seb volunteered. He seemed suddenly eager to be gone, to take the excuse and get out of the room. And, hey, that was fine. If he didn't want to be around, that was no big deal. Trey was fine with it.

But Seb didn't seem to be, because he said, "Actually, Becky, I need to talk to Trey for a couple minutes. Would it be okay if I stayed for a bit? If you wanted to wait in the cafeteria, I could come find you and drive you home later? Or whenever. Whatever you need."

It seemed like Becks was thinking about arguing; she'd been pretty protective all day, driving Trey more-or-less crazy with her fussing. It was nice that she cared, but Trey didn't actually like being treated like a baby. "It's cool, Becks," he said. "I can talk to him. You deserve a break."

She frowned at him, then Seb. "I'll be in the cafeteria. Don't wear him out. The doctor—and your mom, too—said he needs to rest."

"No problem," Seb said. "Thanks."

She left, and Seb stood at the foot of the bed, still looking awkward and unsure.

"What's up?" Trey tried.

Seb took a deep breath, and then the words came out of him fast. "I need to apologize. For—I understand why you were angry yesterday. I took advantage of you—of the situation—and I pushed you into something you weren't into and I am so, so sorry."

Trey tried to sort through it all. Seb was apologizing for—for taking advantage, for pushing... "Are you talking about us fucking?" he asked. It made no sense, but it was all that fit.

And Seb's miserable expression made it seem like a good guess. "I was only thinking about myself. About what *I* like. But obviously if it's not your thing, you'd feel uncomfortable, and I was totally ignoring the power dynamics."

"Wait." The doctors had said he'd likely have some confusion as he recovered from his concussion, but was it supposed to be this bad? "I thought the power thing was the whole point?" He really didn't have the strength for this. "How were you ignoring the power stuff?"

"Not the power in the sex itself—I meant leading up to it. You were a guest in my home, and I pressured you into a—a *fetish*—"

Okay, that was enough to give Trey a little energy. "Jesus, Seb, you didn't pressure me into anything. We fucked. That's all. It was good—totally fine. You've got this built up into something way bigger than it needs to be. I mean—a fetish? I don't even know what that means, really, but if you've got one then so does half the rest of the world. It's totally not weird to like getting pushed around a little. It's weird to get this fucking worked up about it, though."

"Wait." And then Seb closed his eyes, took another deep breath, and opened his eyes again to say, "So why were you angry? Why did you get out of the car, if you weren't angry about this?"

"'Cause you treated me like an idiot! You and Tristan and everybody else, pretending I was at your place to keep you safe, when really it was just another one of Tristan's stupid plans to get me off the street."

Seb stared at him. "Seriously? That's—I mean, we didn't treat you like an idiot! And there *is* a safety issue for me—if you don't believe me, talk to my parents and my bosses—they're all trying to get me to quit this project because they think it's too dangerous. And Tristan and I—if we were manipulating you at all, it's not because we think you're an idiot, it's because you're *stubborn*. I mean, it's completely stupid for you to sleep outside in the cold where people are hunting you when you could be sleeping in a nice warm bed that I'm not using and where you could be helping me to be safe." He shook his head. "Jesus, are you serious? *That's* what you were mad about? I was torturing myself, thinking I'd practically *raped* you, and it turns out—"

"*Raped me*? What the hell?" Trey's head hurt even worse than it had when all this started. "Why would you—I mean, what the—I was the one pushing *you* around. What the hell kind of rape is that?"

"The power imbalance..." Seb seemed much less sure, now, which was a damn good thing.

Trey wished he were at full strength. Hell, he wished he were at half strength. All the same, he managed to get a pretty good glare on and deepened his voice enough to sound at least a bit impressive as he said, "*What* power imbalance?"

Seb took a half-step backward. Shit, Trey liked that. He'd have to be sure to report that to Seb's mom if she came back to check on him again. *"I got kinda turned on when your son looked scared, so I guess* that *part of me is still okay."*

But then Seb took a step forward and said, "No power imbalance. I didn't pressure you into anything. This was all just because—you took off out of my car, put yourself in danger, put *me* in danger, because you didn't like it that people were trying to make sure you were safe? Because people actually cared whether you were okay? Fuck you, Trey. That's a shitty thing to do."

"Oh, no, I'm so sorry, please don't yell at me!" Trey cringed back into his pillows. "Remember the Power Imbalance!"

For a couple seconds Seb just stared at him, and then slowly, reluctantly, he cracked a grin. "Seriously? That's—Jesus. You have no idea how messed up I was about this."

"You're a sensitive fucking flower, I guess."

Trey wished he could keep at it a little longer, but damn, he was tired, and everything hurt. He relaxed back into the pillows and let his eyes drift shut. But his ears still worked, and he knew Seb was coming closer, easing up to the side of the bed.

"You're going to be okay, though—right?" he asked softly.

"I'll be fine," Trey said. It was probably true. His brain *hurt*, but it seemed to work about as well as before the beating. That wasn't saying much, of course, but he'd be able to get by. The doctor had said he'd need surgery on his hand—the fuckers had stomped on it so hard the bones had gotten all moved around into weird places. And a couple ribs were broken, but he'd dealt with that before. The internal bleeding was under control, the doctors said, and that was good, because it had sounded kinda scary. "Broke my cheekbone," he said. "Never broke that before—broke my nose a couple times, but never my cheekbone. They said it hadn't moved, though, so they'll just leave it to heal."

"You look like shit," Seb said. "Your face is all swollen and gross."

"Don't tell me you have a—what did you call it? A *fetish* for that…"

"God, you're an asshole." But Seb sounded relieved, not angry.

Strange how good it made Trey feel to realize that. Strange to realize he gave a damn whether this preppy asshole was mad at him or not. "Go away," he grumbled. Better to end the visit on a positive note. "I'm sleepy."

"And ugly," Seb prompted.

"Not like I was good looking to start with."

"You were alright. And you will be again."

"Not if I don't get my beauty sleep."

"Yeah, okay." Seb shifted back toward the foot of the bed, toward the door, and Trey had the sudden, inexplicable urge to reach out and catch his hand. To ask—no, he didn't want to ask, but if he played his cards right Seb might figure it out for himself. Not that he seemed too good at figuring Trey out so far. But, still. Maybe somehow there was a way to get Seb to sit down in the chair Becky had been sitting in, and he could just hang out for a while. He could watch TV or something while Trey snoozed. That'd be—

No. It'd be a waste of Seb's time. The guy had a million more important things to do, more *fun* things to do. He didn't want to be sitting around in some loser's hospital room.

So Trey didn't catch Seb's hand, didn't ask him to stay, with or without words. He just let him go. And when the door shut behind Seb, Trey tried to pretend he wasn't sorry to be alone.

SEB RAN INTO HIS DAD in the elevator.

"Your friend's okay?" he asked.

"Yeah, I think so. Looks like shit, but still seems to be the same guy. You know, his brain's not—well, not any more scrambled than it was before all this."

"That's a relief." And he sounded like he meant it. He *did* mean it. If there was anything Seb knew about his dad—about both of his parents—it was that they were genuinely caring people. They'd proved it over and over, showing compassion to others, teaching their kids about social responsibility and giving back to the community—they were good people.

And they wanted their kids to be good people, too. He needed to remember that for the conversation to come.

His mom was in a meeting when the two of them arrived at her office, so they sat in the armchairs outside and waited. Well, they waited for about thirty seconds, and then Seb said, "I'm not going to quit. I understand why you're worried and I appreciate your concern. We can talk about some ways to make things safer, if you want, or ways to help you understand why this is important to me. But I'm not going to quit."

His dad looked toward his wife's office door as if willing it to open up. He wasn't weak, Seb knew; he was totally capable of making his own decisions. But he was also pretty dedicated to the co-parenting, teamwork approach. "We should wait for your mom," he said.

"Okay. Maybe she'll have some good ideas about how to keep me safe; I'm totally interested in hearing those. I'm not trying to be reckless or anything. But I'm not going to let some goons intimidate me. This is Seattle, not Mogadishu. We have police here, and a good legal system."

"Have the police found anything on this yet?"

Damn. "Not that I've heard about. But that doesn't mean they won't."

"And you have reason to believe they're investigating it seriously?"

"Yeah, of course!" At least, Seb hoped they were.

"Then why not leave it to them?" His father waited a moment to let Seb see the trap he'd stumbled into. "If our system is safe and fair and effective, then there's no need for you to be involved; you're redundant. If our system *isn't* safe and fair and effective, then you shouldn't be involved because it's too dangerous."

"It's not black and white," Seb tried. "There's no such thing as *absolutely* safe, or absolutely fair and effective. Right? So... this is quite a safe city, and fair and effective..." He wasn't sure if he wanted to bring up the next part. He felt hypocritical, somehow, criticizing a system that had helped him so much. But maybe it was all the help he'd gotten that made him the one who *should* be criticizing it. "At least it's fair and effective for us. For—you know. For people with money and education and connections and all the rest. People with reliable cars to get them places and safe apartments in secure buildings to come home to. People the police respect and want to help. For us—for *me*—it's safe and fair. But for other people? It's honestly not working out for them, Dad."

There was something unreadable in his father's expression, something Seb couldn't remember having seen before. He didn't have time to do much analysis, though, before his mother's office door opened and two men in white medical coats stepped out, looking like they weren't entirely pleased but weren't going to start bitching until they were safely out of their boss's earshot. His mother appeared in their wake and smiled warmly.

"You're both here." She waited for them to stand up and walk to the office door, then kissed Seb on the cheek and took her husband's hand.

Such a warm, cozy family. Something that Seb usually took for granted, or was embarrassed about, but now, thinking of Trey lying all alone in his hospital room, he resolved to be more appreciative. At least if they stopped trying to tell him what to do.

"So I've already explained my position to Dad," he said as they moved into the office. "I think he's coming around. Now I just have to make you understand, and we're all set." He sank into a leather easy-chair, leaned back and laced his hands behind his head, and gave her his most confident grin. "Where should I begin?"

Chapter Fourteen

THE BAD THING ABOUT BEING in the hospital was—well, everything about being in the hospital was bad. But the *worst* thing was feeling trapped. Trey wasn't even sure he was getting any medicine through the needle in his arm; it seemed like it might just be one more way of keeping him from being able to move around. He had no clothes, no money, didn't really know where he was, felt like shit, *and* they had him taped up to some stupid bag of clear goo that didn't seem at all mobile. It was bullshit, and he wanted to yell at someone about it, but they all seemed way too efficient, too important, too damn clean and smart and professional for him to take on.

So he lay in his bed and he stewed, all through that second night—the first one he was conscious for—and into the next morning. Becky'd told him the night before that she had to work and wouldn't be able to visit, and he hadn't thought he'd mind. It might be nice to have some peace and time to himself, he'd thought. But by nine-thirty in the morning, when he heard the gentle knock on the door to his room, he had to admit it to himself—he was lonesome, and he wanted some company.

When Seb's head appeared, peeking around the door with a strange show of respect for privacy, considering how much of each other they'd already seen naked, Trey would have jumped out of bed to give him a big hug, if he wasn't so effectively constrained. And if he'd been somebody else, the kind of person who gave big hugs to people.

As it was, he grunted a sort of greeting. "You taking time off work?"

"That's an interesting question," Seb said. He eased into the chair beside Trey's bed, then frowned and stood back up. "You need stools or something in here. It's weird to be so low when I'm trying to talk to you."

"So ask your mom for one—she's the Big Cheese, right?"

Seb shrugged. "She's a fair-sized cheese, I guess, but she still has to report to people. It's not like she *owns* the hospital or anything."

"Is that a thing? Do people actually own hospitals?"

"Uh—sometimes. Not usually just one person, though."

Interesting. If Trey ever had that kind of money he could think of about a billion things he'd buy instead of a hospital, but it wasn't like he ever *was* going to have that kind of money, so he didn't need to worry about how to spend it.

But there was *something* Trey was worried about, or at least curious about. "So, what's a support person? What's that mean?"

Seb stared at him blankly for a moment, then jerked his head as if he'd just realized what Trey was talking about. "That's the term I had to use to get the hospital to tell me—so I could tell everyone—how you were. It's just a term; I don't think it really means anything."

Right. Of course it didn't. "Oh, okay."

Trey thought about turning the TV on, or doing something else to direct Seb's attention elsewhere. But he wasn't quick enough, and Seb said, "Why? Where'd you hear it?"

"Oh, just one of—I think he was a social worker, maybe? Somebody who works for the hospital. He was just trying to figure out where I'd be going when I got out of here."

"Are they talking about releasing you soon?"

"Maybe tomorrow? I have to talk to the brain guys first, but if they say I'm okay then they can fix up my hand this afternoon. And then I'm good to go."

"What about the internal bleeding? And your face?"

"The bleeding's stopped, they say. And my face—it's just my face. There's no point taking up a hospital bed just for a messed up face."

"Wow. Okay, great." But Seb didn't look like it was great—not at all.

"It's not a big deal," Trey said. "The 'support person' thing, or whatever. Like you said, it's just a word you used to get some information. It doesn't mean you actually have to, like, *support* me."

"No, I—" Seb stopped, frowned, almost spoke, frowned even more deeply, then shook his head. "Shit. I wasn't going to tell you about this yet. *We* weren't—Tristan and the rest of them agreed it wasn't something you needed to worry about. But if you're getting out, you should know about it."

"Know about what?" Trey asked the question because he was supposed to be a grown man who wanted to be in charge, not a little kid who wanted to hide. But he wasn't looking forward to the answer.

"Things have changed." Seb made a face. "The Communities Team pulled the plug on any direct action. They'll support us— you guys—whatever. They'll offer support if we can find grounds for a legal challenge. But if we're sticking to the get-people-stirred-up-and-get-public-opinion-on-our-side approach, they're out."

"Out? They were barely *in*." Except... oh. "But you're not working with us anymore. That's what this means?"

"No. I'm not working with *them* anymore." Seb shrugged. "My parents aren't too enthusiastic about it, but they're not threatening to disown me or anything, so it's not like I actually need the pay from the internship. I was doing it as a way to network and get some experience, but, fuck it. I don't want to build a network of cowards, and I can get good experience with you guys."

It seemed important somehow. Seemed like a bigger deal than Seb was making it out to be. "You really think you're picking the right side on this one?"

"Yeah," Seb said quietly. "I don't know if it'll be the winning side, but you getting beat up makes it more clear than ever that it's the *right* side."

Trey kind of wanted to think about it all for a while, to let it roll around in his brain so he could figure out what fit in where. But Seb didn't have all day to sit around and watch Trey try to understand. "So how does that make things different, for me getting out?"

"We've been having little meetings—only one with the full group, but lots of smaller teams. And we think we want to kick things into gear. We can't just sit around on the defensive, expecting everyone to be on their guard all the time forever. So we're putting a big push on. Simon and I are getting closer to the names behind the companies that own the real estate—they're really well-hidden, but in a way that's actually *good*, because it means they don't want their names associated with this in any way. They wouldn't have gone to the trouble of setting up all the holding companies and foreign registrations and all the rest if they didn't really want anonymity. So we're going to go public—a big rally, as much publicity as we can come up with, the whole show. If we can make it clear that we're *not* going to shut up, then they'll get scared and we hope they'll back down."

"Or gear up," Trey said. "I need to get out of here so I can help protect people." He looked down at the IV still in his arm and wondered how bad it would be if he just pulled it out. He'd take a punch to the face without fear, but something about the idea of that tiny needle slicing around inside him—well, too bad. His people needed him. He reached for the tape holding it all still, but Seb's hand caught his.

"What the hell are you doing? You're—" He shook his head. "You can't think you're leaving here, not right now and not because of what's going on outside. You're on the bench for this, Trey. That's why we weren't going to tell you about it, because we knew you'd get all worked up. But you're hurt. Staying in the hospital was going to keep you safe, but if that isn't going to happen, you need to come to my place—without any of your whining and bullshit about not wanting us to take care of you, because shut up with that—and lie around and *get better*."

"I'm already better. That's why they're letting me out of the hospital." That and his total inability to pay any of the bills he was sure were expanding like a bag of popcorn in the microwave. But for some reason, no one had been in to harass him about any of that yet, so he didn't need to mention it to Seb.

"Your ribs are broken," Seb scolded. "You know what your ribs are? They're the protective cage for all the organs that *keep you alive*. You know what your cheekbone does, when it's not broken? It protects your eye, and your brain and the part of your face that does your fucking *breathing*. Your armor is smashed up, man, and you can't go back into battle until it's repaired."

In a different context Trey would really like the idea of being a well-armored warrior, but right then it just sounded like another excuse for keeping him from being useful. Still, he didn't fight to free himself from Seb's light grip. Didn't pull his arm back, either. Just because he wanted to keep the rip-out-the-needle option open, not because he wanted to hold hands or anything.

And maybe Seb was worried he might go back to trying to remove the needle, because he didn't let go either. He did scowl, though, and say, "I need—not just me, obviously. Tristan and Becky and all the rest of them, *they* need to know you're safe. No more of your bullshit running away—when people are worried about you, it's an asshole move to make them *more* worried. So you'll stay at my place, and I've already talked to the team about doing more work over there instead of at Tristan's because it's a more secure building, so you can be part of that, if you want, but the rest of it?"

"What are you doing?" Trey asked quietly, and he did pull his hand away now because he needed to have his full concentration available to pay attention to this conversation. "You've known us for, like, a week. And you're this involved? You're inviting me to stay with you again, and you want them all doing work at your place? You quit your fucking job, and, yeah, okay, I get that you don't need the money, but all the same—what are you doing? Or— not what. *Why*. Why are you doing it?"

Seb let his hand fall to his lap and looked down at it like he thought the answer might be written on his palm. Then he lifted his head. "I'm not sure. I think—I think it's about me, not about you. Any of you. If that makes sense? I think—do you ever feel as if there are times in your life that are just more important, somehow? Like, decisions you make, or *don't* make, that will affect how the whole rest of your life goes? Not just your life, but *you* in your life?" He wrinkled his face up, clearly frustrated by his inability to put his thoughts into words Trey would be able to understand.

But Trey was pretty sure he *did* understand. "Like a gut check. A test. If you do one thing, you're going to be one kind of person—the kind of person who does that kind of thing. And if you do the other thing you'll be another kind of person. Forever."

Seb's smile was pure and beautiful. "Yeah. Exactly that. I feel like if I turn my back on this now, if I walk away and go back to my comfortable life, then I'm going to *always* be the kind of person who turns his back and walks away from other people's trouble. And I don't want to be that kind of person."

"There's got to be a middle ground, though." Trey wasn't sure why he was making an argument against his own interests—maybe his brain was more scrambled than he'd thought. "You could, like, help out in smaller ways, without inviting some ugly loser into your house."

Seb frowned at him. "Tristan's not that ugly."

Trey snorted. Nice try. "What are your neighbors going to say? You thought about that? If they see my beat-up ass coming and going from your place?"

"No, you're not going to come and *go*, asshole. Remember? You're going to come and *stay*. You're going to get some sleep and eat some soup—my mom makes soup when she's stressed, and I've got a freezer full of really good shit—and hang out and get better. And then by the time you're feeling better and your face isn't so messed up? Oh, wait, by that time I *still* won't give a shit what my neighbors think."

"It's that easy?"

Seb nodded. "Yeah. You staying at my place? Totally easy. The rest of it? Harder. But we'll figure it out. Okay?"

It was the perfect answer. Probably too perfect, and Trey shouldn't trust it, but he was tired and he hurt. The hospital was creepy and he wanted out, but he didn't want to go sleep in the park, or even on Tristan's couch. Not when he could be in Seb's warm, comfy bed.

Wait, no, not *Seb's* bed. That wasn't going to happen. Seb was offering charity, not sex.

"Okay," Trey said. Charity, yes. But he was tired, and sore, and there was something about the way Seb offered his help that made it seem okay to accept. Maybe Trey would regret it later; hell, of course he would. But that was a problem for another day.

Kate Sherwood

Chapter Fifteen

SEB HAD SEEN INTERNET VIDEOS of adult dogs trying to teach puppies how to manage stairs. Good natured and willing, but kind of confused about what the problem was and absolutely baffled about the best way to help. After trying to herd Trey out of the hospital, into the car, and then up to his apartment, Seb could absolutely relate to the adult dogs.

None of it should have been as complicated as it was.

Well, that wasn't fair. Some of it was tricky because Trey was clearly hurting. But it was frustrating that he wouldn't *admit* he was hurting, and went to such ridiculous lengths to disguise a reality everyone was clearly aware of. He could have asked for help getting his shoes tied up, but instead he'd figured out some weird system of shoving the laces inside the shoes before dropping them to the floor and pushing his feet into them and had then said that was how he wore his shoes. Didn't tie them, liked them loose. It was such bullshit, but Seb let it go because it didn't seem like a battle worth fighting.

But possibly he should have had the showdown then and spared himself some of the later absurdity. Trey bitching about having to be in a wheelchair and then trying to wheel it himself, even though he'd just had surgery on his hand the day before and had his whole arm in a sling. He'd rammed into two different carts in the hallway before Seb had growled at him and taken over, just like that golden retriever who'd picked the pup up by his head and carried him up the stairs.

The puppy had at least seemed grateful. Trey had bitched that Seb drove like a grandma and needed to get moving.

The whole check-out process, really, had felt like a furtive escape, and Seb wondered if Trey understood that he wasn't going to get hit with a bill for his care. Between the social worker and Seb's mom it had been taken care of, and Seb knew Trey'd been told that, but maybe he didn't believe it?

Or maybe he was being a pain in the ass for a totally different reason. There were no bills to worry about when they got to the car, but Trey still insisted on climbing into the passenger seat without any help—maybe Seb should have borrowed his Mom's Mercedes instead of driving his own too-high SUV—and then swatted Seb away instead of letting him help with the seatbelt. Bitching about Seb's careful driving on the way home was only forgivable when Seb looked over and saw how drawn and grey Trey's face was. He had his head pressed against the glass of the passenger window, his eyes closed, his jaw clenched. He was in pain, probably, but—

"If you're going to puke, you need to give me some warning, okay? I can pull over, but there's traffic—"

"I'm not going to puke," Trey said. His voice was too small, and Seb tried to find a way to still drive without any jarring while also driving *faster*.

Trey perked up by the time they got to the apartment, insisted he was fine taking the stairs, only accepted that they'd be taking the freight elevator because Seb refused to unlock the stairwell door, and then staggered so hard on the way to the elevator that Seb had to grab him to keep him upright—and, of course, managed to press against his broken ribs in the process.

By the time they were upstairs they were both drained, although Seb was the only one willing to admit it.

"Go to your room," he ordered. "Watch TV, or go to sleep. If you think you'll stay awake, I can thaw some soup for you." He checked his watch. "Wait. It's a bit early for your painkillers, but not much. If you want, you can have them now and they'll help you sleep."

"You're not the drug police," Trey said. "I'll take my pills when I want to."

Another fight Seb needed to avoid. "Okay. Do you want to take some now?"

Trey glared at him. Then he pressed his lips together and cast his eyes toward the floor like a shamed—well, yeah, like a shamed puppy. "I'm an asshole," he mumbled.

"Yup," Seb agreed easily. "You're also swaying on your feet so bad you're making me seasick. Go lie down, asshole, and I'll bring you your pills. You can decide for yourself if you want them."

And Trey didn't argue. Seb wasn't naive enough to think the tractability was going to last, but he enjoyed it while he could. A couple minutes later he went into the bedroom and found Trey sprawled out on top of the covers, shoes still on, dead to the world. Seb quietly set the pills and four bottles of liquid—one straight water, two different flavoured varieties, one Gatorade—on the bedside table. He eased Trey's shoes off, finally glad they weren't properly tied, and pulled the comforter from the other side of the bed over Trey.

And then, god help him, he almost crawled into bed beside him. Was he going to fucking *spoon* the guy? Was that what he was thinking? Just snuggle up for an evening nap? Or even worse, was he thinking he'd be staying there the whole night?

He practically ran out of the room and shut the door firmly behind himself. Trey was there because he needed a safe, warm bed. Not because Seb *wanted* him there—not because Seb *wanted* him at all. One fuck, one BJ, and a lot of bickering was not the start of a relationship, and that was a damn good thing because Seb wasn't looking for a relationship. Certainly not with—

He caught himself. *Not with someone like Trey.* That was what he'd been thinking. Those exact words had been in his head.

Someone like Trey. Seb had meant someone stubborn and aggressive, not—it hadn't been a *class* thing, hadn't been about how impossible it was to imagine Trey, rough and uneducated, sitting down for a nice family dinner at the Tanner residence or drinking craft beer with Brock and the other cousins. No, Seb hadn't gotten nearly that far in his imaginings, so it couldn't be what he was reacting against.

Not consciously, at least.

But subconsciously. Shit.

No, it didn't matter. At least, not right then, not in relation to Trey. Seb should do some soul-searching at some point, likely, should dig out some of his feelings on all this and examine them more closely, but he didn't need to do it for Trey. Because Trey was just a house guest. Just someone who needed somewhere to stay.

There was no more to it than that, so there was no need for Seb to go looking for trouble.

~*~*~*~

TREY WOKE UP GROGGY. There was sunlight coming in the bedroom window—it was morning? He shifted carefully and the stabs of agony from his ribs helped him remember. Right. A restless night, shifting around trying to find a comfortable position, a grateful swallow of the two pills and liquid left on his bedside table, some more sleep—seemed like that was his life these days.

He heard a gentle murmur of sound from somewhere else in the apartment. The place seemed pretty well sound-proofed, so if it was loud enough for him to hear it at all, it was full-volume out there. But full-volume what? No, it was clearly conversation, so the real question was full-volume *who*?

He eased his way to the side of the bed and glanced wistfully at the little table where he'd found his pills the night before. Too bad Seb hadn't left the whole bottle—but there were two more pills there now.

Better to resent the way Seb was taking control of things, or appreciate the consideration he'd shown, sneaking in to check on Trey and leave the pills behind?

Best to just swallow the painkillers with a shot of blue Gatorade and not think about any of the rest of it.

Trey sat on the edge of the bed for a few minutes after that, trying to regroup, build his strength, develop a plan—something. The only thing that came to him was that he needed to piss, so he staggered to the bathroom, took care of that, and then cautiously opened the bedroom door.

He still couldn't see what was going on, but he could hear better, and that was enough to let him relax. Tristan, Simon, probably others, but they all sounded easy and friendly, not the way they would if there were strangers in the mix. So Trey took another couple steps down the hall, then froze as he understood what they were talking about.

"He's going to want to help," Tristan was saying. "He's got to be hurting, but he's too damn stubborn to let that show, so he'll just get pissed off if we try to slow him down."

"You know him better than I do," Seb responded. "But—he was really mad when he thought we were manipulating him before. I thought it was something else, but it turns out it was just that he thought we weren't giving him the full story, and he hated it. I mean, he's not stupid. He'll figure it out if you trick him. And— it's not respectful, you know? It's coming from a good place. I get that. But, I don't know—maybe he used to be more stubborn than he is now? No, that's not right, he's still totally stubborn. But is it possible that maybe he's grown up a bit and he can do a better job of deciding *when* to be stubborn? You've known him for a long time, but—maybe that means you still see him like he used to be, and maybe he isn't completely that way anymore. Are you still the exact same person you were when you first met him?"

There was a gap in the conversation then, and Trey tried to figure out if they were actually thinking it through or just working out a polite way to tell Seb he didn't know what he was talking about.

Except—what if he *did* know what he was talking about? Was Trey the same guy he'd been when he first met Tristan and the rest of them? There were some similarities, sure. He was still going nowhere, still the dumb one, and damn it, he was still the tough one, whatever the rest of them thought. But maybe he *had* grown up a little? He'd been an asshole to Seb the night before, but at least he'd admitted it. Didn't that count for anything?

And Seb was speaking up for Trey now, and damn it, that *absolutely* counted for something. So Trey carefully stepped backward until he reached the bedroom door, then pulled it shut loud enough that it would be heard, but he hoped not loud enough to be obvious that he was announcing his presence.

"Seb?" he called, and cleared his throat when he heard how creaky his voice sounded. Of course, the throat-clearing was close enough to a cough to send his ribs into spasms of agony, and by the time his head stopped swimming from that, Seb was in view at the end of the short hallway.

"Hey, man. You okay?"

"I'm sore," Trey said. Loud enough that the jerks in the living room could hear him. There, he'd done it. He'd admitted his weakness, shown his growth, proved Seb right—it was enough. But from nowhere, without even meaning to, he added, "Thanks for setting the pills out for me. It hurt bad enough last night I probably would have gulped the whole bottle if they'd all been in there."

"No problem," Seb said, and the caution in his tone made it clear he was looking for the trap. Made it clear Seb really didn't think Trey had changed all *that* much.

And, fuck it, Seb was right about that. "So where's my breakfast, bitch? I don't want that oatmeal crap you gave me last time. Have you got, like, eggs or waffles or anything?"

"Nope," Seb said cheerfully. "I've got oatmeal crap, or yogurt crap... if you're feeling non-traditional I can heat you up some soup, but if you call that crap we'll have a problem, 'cause nobody insults my mom's soup. Got it?"

"Is Tristan here? I thought I heard his voice. Can he make me pancakes? Do you have the stuff for them?"

"I don't even know what pancake ingredients would be. I think I have flour..." Seb backed up a couple steps and angled his body to make the invitation forward clear. "Come sit down before you fall down. Sir Tristan and I will consult on your culinary demands, my liege."

Trey liked the sound of that. He let himself be herded into the main room and nodded his greetings to Tristan, Simon, and Noah, then sank carefully into an overstuffed leather chair. He probably should have stayed standing because it was going to be a bitch to get back to his feet.

But he wouldn't have to do that for a while. Maybe he could just sit there with everyone bustling around him and taking care of him and he could just let that happen. This was real life, so Seb was in charge. If they ever fucked again, Trey would be in charge, and that would be absolutely fine. More than fine.

But in real life, Seb wanted Trey to sit quietly, so Trey sat quietly. Even the demands he was making, he was making because he had the feeling Seb wanted him to; the oatmeal had been fine, really, and it would have been a lot easier to chew than anything else. But Seb wanted something to fuss over, and Seb was in charge. So let him fuss over breakfast, and different flavors of water on the bedside table and whatever else. It was Seb's show.

And for whatever reason, Trey was totally okay with that.

~*~*~*~

IT WAS STRANGE HAVING PEOPLE in his apartment. People Seb was going to see again the next day, rather than just random tricks. It should have felt like an invasion, but it didn't.

He supposed he didn't feel like he had to keep secrets from these visitors. Tristan used to be a prostitute, Simon had apparently been connected to organized crime, and Noah—well, Noah was pretty pure, but he didn't seem to have an issue with anyone else's idiosyncrasies, so there was no reason to think he'd object to Seb's.

And it wouldn't matter if he did. That was part of it. Seb liked these guys, but he obviously loved his family more, was obviously more concerned about not disappointing them. Not *disgusting* them. If these guys found out something they didn't like and walked away, it wouldn't be a big deal. At least, it wouldn't be a big deal if most of them walked. And Trey already knew and hadn't seemed too alarmed—hell, the smug bastard hadn't thought it was a big deal at all.

And so, for the first time since Seb had moved into the apartment, he was able to relax with friends in his space.

Relax emotionally, at least. Mentally was another issue, because first he had to figure out what the hell to serve Princess Trey for breakfast, and when that was resolved—via a no-eggs pancake recipe Tristan found on his phone—there was the actual business that had brought the guys to the apartment.

"The permits should be lined up by this afternoon," Simon said. "We've got the route mapped out, and almost a week to get people excited for it. Seb, you've got the press release written up?"

Seb nodded. "Yeah. And I've contacted the *Times* and the weeklies and the TV and radio stations."

"I've got a good start on the social media stuff," Noah said. "And I talked to some people at school. It sucks that it's summer time—a lot of the student groups are shut down until fall. But there was *some* interest, at least."

"I talked to the nurses at the hospital," Trey rumbled. "They're totally on our side, and they're having a bake sale to raise money."

Everyone turned to look at him and he shrugged. "Okay, no, I didn't do that. Technically."

"You had other things on your mind," Tristan said. "But—" He looked at Seb and shrugged.

Passing the baton. Tagging himself out, and Seb in. How the hell had that happened? Seb had been appointed Trey-handler? Seriously?

Well, he supposed he'd sort of appointed himself, when he'd disagreed with Tristan's suggested approach earlier. So he'd asked for this. He took a deep breath and then exhaled. "We think maybe you should be a more prominent part of things now, if you're willing."

"What?"

"The other victims are—I mean, the ones from the fire are *dead*. The vet from the animal shelter is speaking up, and she's great in front of the cameras, but there's no real proof that fire was connected to the real estate stuff. There's no *proof* the other fire was connected, either. But for you? The guys *told you* why they were going after you. They told *me*, on the phone. The guy said you'd been warned. The cops might not be doing much about that, but I think the media might be interested. And if they aren't we can do it ourselves—put a video together and get it on the internet, work to get it out there."

"A video of *me*." Trey sounded like he was waiting for the punchline.

"I know it's not your thing. If you're not at all comfortable talking to a reporter, then we can go with the homemade version and slap it on YouTube or something—but local media would be really valuable. The internet's good at getting things out across the globe, but it's not actually going to do us much good if some guy in Peru is worked up about this situation. We need the attention right here in Seattle so we can pressure the local authorities to help us."

"And you actually think it's going to get us attention—*good* attention—if people hear me talking? Are you high right now?"

"Jesus, Trey, you're not a monster. I mean, you look pretty rough right now, and, yeah, we'd want to coach you a bit before an interview—like, for example, you shouldn't ask the reporter if he or she is *high*—but you can totally do this. And the way you look is an asset, really. It makes it clear how serious these guys were."

"If your Community Team guys were still involved, they wouldn't be suggesting this."

"No, probably not," Seb admitted. "They don't seem all that big on taking chances. But they're *not* involved, so who the hell cares what they think?"

Trey frowned at him. "You're serious about this. You really think I can do it?"

"Absolutely," Seb said. And it was true, mostly. Trey *could* do this. On a good day, if the reporter asked the right questions in the right way and Trey didn't get flustered and aggressive and absolutely nothing went wrong, he could totally do it. "If you want to. It's worth a try, we think."

Trey's gaze travelled around the room, then returned to Seb. It was too much damn responsibility all of a sudden. Trey was asking for guidance, and who the hell was Seb to offer it to him? How arrogant was he to think he had the answers, how reckless with someone else's trust?

"You don't have to do it," he said quickly. "If you don't think it's a good idea, we'll figure something else out."

"It'd be useful, though? If I could do it—if you guys could coach me through it and tell me what to say and how to say it—it would help?"

"We think it would," Tristan said, and Seb was more than glad of the interruption. The sharing of the burden.

Still, it was Seb Trey looked at as he said, "Okay, then. I'll do it."

And that was that. Trey hadn't just made a decision; he'd somehow created an obligation. Trey was trusting Seb, so now Seb had to be worthy of that trust.

It should have felt like a weight, a restraint, and in a way, it did. But it was surprising how comfortable it was, being tied to Trey.

Chapter Sixteen

IT ALL TURNED INTO A KIND of routine after that. Trey would mope around the apartment and bitch about stupid things, then go to sleep, and when he woke up Seb would be there with drugs and soup and patience.

The rest of the gang was there a lot, too—it seemed like headquarters had been officially shifted from Tristan's place to Seb's—but somehow they were all just background noise. Not unpleasant, but not important. Becky snuggled up to Trey just like she always had, and he was happy to have the warmth and the contact, as long as she remembered to be easy on his bruises. But instead of sinking into the cocoon the two of them had tended to form in the past, he felt like he was always pulling away from it, craning his head to keep an eye or an ear on whatever Seb was doing.

"You know you can't trust him, right?" Becks asked on the third day as the others were busy with their own conversations. Her voice was low, but Seb might have been able to hear her, if he'd been paying as much attention to Trey as Trey was to him. But of course he wasn't—he was busy laughing at something Noah had said over at the big dining table.

"I know," Trey replied, not bothering to pretend he didn't understand her.

"He's not one of us. It's not his fault, just like it's not our fault. But you know that story with the scorpion and the frog. The scorpion talks the frog into giving him a ride across the river, saying that of course he won't sting, because then the frog wouldn't be able to carry him and he'd drown. So the frog agrees and halfway across the scorpion stings him. They start drowning and the frog gasps, *why*?"

"And the scorpion says he couldn't help himself—it's his nature." Yeah, Trey knew the story. He'd never liked it much, but he knew it.

But Becky seemed to think it was pretty significant. "Messing with rich people? Sooner or later, you're going to get stung and you'll drown. It's just in their nature."

As Trey remembered the story, both the frog *and* the scorpion had drowned, but he didn't bother pointing that out to Becky. She wouldn't really care about the fate of the scorpion, after all. Not like Trey did.

"I know," he repeated instead.

She frowned at him, then twisted around so she could run her fingers gently through his hair. "I don't want you to get hurt." This time her voice was low enough that nobody but him had a chance of hearing it.

"I don't want it either. But..." But what could he do?

Her fingers stopped stroking and rubbed his head more vigorously. "Okay," she agreed. "Sometimes you just have to ride it out. And I'll keep an eye on you—maybe I'll be able to pull you out of the river."

"I'm pretty heavy. Make sure you don't end up getting dragged in." And then, because there was only so much of this poetic bullshit any self-respecting thug could withstand, he half-rolled away from her and patted his stomach. "Not quite as heavy as I used to be." In a louder voice he announced, "My soup-bitch is trying to starve me skinny. Sure would be nice if I had some of that curried chicken stuff from last night. Yeah, that'd be really tasty about now."

Noah frowned over at him. "You seriously can't walk to the kitchen and put soup in the microwave?"

But Seb was already moving. "He's got to reserve his strength for the big interview."

Trey groaned. He'd agreed to it, and he'd do it. But it was going to be a disaster, obviously. If he got lucky his concussion would act up and he could go back to the hospital for a while, and he wouldn't have to talk to the reporter.

"You want toast again?" Seb called from the kitchen.

"Nah," Trey replied. Of course he wanted toast, or anything solid and filling, but it had hurt to eat it the night before, each movement as he chewed sending pain up through his face. He wasn't going to admit that, though, especially not in front of Noah, who would absolutely report the weakness to Shane.

But when Seb came out with the soup, there was a plate of toast on the tray beside it, cut into long, thin strips. "Thought you might want to dip them in the soup," Seb said casually. Nothing for Noah to notice or bother repeating. "They'd get a bit soggy, but that's not the end of the world."

A tiny part of Trey wanted to rebel. This was Seb manipulating again, Seb ignoring what Trey had clearly said in favor of what Seb, in his maturity and wisdom, thought was best. Trey should make a stand. Maybe not throw the toast back in Seb's face, but at least not eat it. He'd *said* he didn't want it.

But it smelled really good, and if it was soaked in soup it'd be easy to eat.

It was probably the first step—or, hell, not the first one, just one more of many steps—down a path he'd regret, but Trey nodded as Seb set the tray on the end table next to him. "Thanks," he grunted.

Seb smiled at him, and Trey smiled back despite himself, despite the complaints from his cheek and his head. Yeah, taking the toast hadn't been any kind of a first step. Trey was a good way down this path, and there was no turning around now. He might as well just relax and enjoy the view, at least until he tripped over whatever landmine was going to destroy it all.

~*~*~*~

TREY WAS ASLEEP AND THE apartment was otherwise empty when Seb found it. He'd been looking over the latest documents they'd dug up, sorting through the maze of shell corporations and foreign ownership and other financial sleight-of-hand, when his eyes snagged on something too familiar. His whole body froze—*time* froze—and he stared at the company name, unable to look away.

Allistian Holdings.

The familiar mix of his sister's name and his own. His father had loved that, when he'd explained it to them.

Seb never paid much attention to his father's business operations. He played the market with the substantial fortune he'd inherited from his family, and that was all.

But he'd set up a holding company for Allison and Seb, too, with enough invested in it to pay for their day-to-day expenses and still leave enough left over for the fund to grow.

Allistian Holdings. A majority shareholder in a numbered corporation, and that numbered corporation held shares in a real estate investment partnership based in Zurich, and that real estate investment partnership owned several smaller corporations, one of which owned another company that owned—

Seb didn't want to believe it. He needed to sort through it all again, make sure he hadn't missed something, or transposed some numbers somewhere or—

But already he was coming up with excuses: It was all too remote. It wasn't as if he and Allison owned that much of the property in Trey's old neighborhood. And they didn't own *any* of it, outright. He certainly didn't have any decision making power—not that he was aware of, at least. None of it was in his name.

No. Not in his name, not directly. But his name, combined with Allison's, was there in the paper trail.

Not clear enough that anyone else would be likely to spot it, not unless they dug even deeper than Seb had.

And who was going to do that? Simon had the skills, certainly, but he was spending most of his time on organizing the protest, getting the permits and rallying the residents and making sure everyone else was doing their parts. Tristan? No, he got frustrated after only a few minutes of sorting through all the records. Noah had put his time in, but he didn't have the background in business to really know what he was looking at.

Seb was the only one who'd found this, and he was the only one who was likely to.

But for some reason that realization did nothing to ease the churning in his chest. Even if no one else found out, he'd still know.

He stared at the screen for another long moment, then turned off the computer and checked his phone. Ten thirty. His dad was an early-to-bed, early-to-rise type, and there was no way he'd still be awake.

Seb hesitated. Was there anything to be gained by waking his father up? What could the poor guy possibly say that would make this better? Was Seb a man or was he a child, running to his daddy for comfort and explanation?

Was there anything about this that couldn't wait until morning?

Seb knew his dad turned off his ringer when he went to sleep, so it was safe to text. *I need to talk to you about Allistian. As soon as possible. Can I meet you tomorrow first thing?*

He hit send.

Then he sat there at his dining room table—the table his mother had bought for him—and looked around the condo—one more investment his parents had made for him, for his benefit, and that he'd never bothered to really consider in any larger context— and the home that he'd thought of as his sanctuary began to feel like something else altogether. Had he been hiding here because he wanted to maintain his privacy, or because he'd wanted to hide from reality? From guilt?

No, he hadn't known. But he should have.

And now that he did, he needed to do something about it.

Chapter Seventeen

SEB WASN'T HOME WHEN TREY dragged his ass out of bed the next morning. He must have gone out to pick up coffee or something. He'd be back soon.

And how ridiculous was it that Trey had to tell himself that, had to try to fucking *comfort* himself, like he was a kid getting left at kindergarten for the first time. Seb had gone out because Seb had a damn life that involved things a hell of a lot more important than fussing over Trey. That was all.

Still, it was weird to be in the guy's space when he wasn't around. Tempting to explore a little, maybe check out what kind of kinky shit Seb had in his bedroom—but, no, that wouldn't be cool. If Trey ever got to see any of that stuff it would be because Seb had invited him, not because he'd snuck in.

He was trying to figure out how Seb's fancy coffee maker worked when the screen that controlled the downstairs door beeped.

Shit. Was he supposed to answer that? What if it was one of Seb's friends, or a member of his family? He had a sister, he'd said—Trey sure didn't want to have to explain his presence to some unfamiliar rich girl. But Seb's mom had known Trey was going home with Seb, hadn't she?

And it might be one of the team, or Seb himself. How much of a loser would Trey look like if he was sitting around in the apartment, listening to the damn buzzer going without doing a thing about it, and if it was Seb himself, coming back from wherever he'd been and for some reason unable to enter his own code....

The panel buzzed again and Trey strode toward it like he knew what he was doing. He jabbed at the *view* button and got a pretty good closeup of a forehead that looked vaguely familiar.

"Simon?"

The forehead moved back, and Simon's face became clear. "Trey? Buzz me up—the news guys are going to be here any minute."

"What? This morning? No, Seb thought tomorrow, maybe!"

"Yeah, but they want to do it earlier, and we can't afford to say no. Where *is* Seb?"

"I don't know." Trey thought about refusing to let Simon in. Could he say it wouldn't be right, with Seb not home? Sure, Seb had thought it was a great idea to have the reporter come to the condo, but he'd thought he'd be there to supervise. Trey couldn't take advantage of his hospitality, couldn't just start letting strangers come in whenever they wanted—

"Trey!" Simon said, his voice a little sharper. "Buzz me up."

So Trey hit the button.

Then he paced. Where the hell was Seb? How long did it take to buy coffee, or whatever he was doing? Not getting coffee, Trey realized; there was plenty in the kitchen. But he hadn't mentioned any errands the night before, so it had to be something unplanned.

No note, he determined after a quick scan of the logical spots.

It was stupid how nervous he felt. It was just Simon coming up, and Seb would be back before the interview, for sure. He wouldn't have left Trey alone for too long without warning him— would he?

Maybe he doesn't realize what a pathetic loser you are. Maybe he thinks you're old enough to be on your own for a few damn hours so he can get stuff done. Maybe he's sick of your ugly, beat-up face and your stupid talking and he couldn't stand the idea of dealing with you again today. Maybe he's hoping you'll get the message and be packed up and gone by the time he gets back. Maybe this whole thing was just a big misunderstanding and he never wanted you to stay here at all. Maybe—

The banging on the hallway door was a merciful interruption to that train of thought, but it was hard to be truly happy to see Simon when he stalked in with such a glower on his face.

"Where the hell is Seb? I called him twice and left a message both times. Texted him—no answer. Where is he?"

And, shit, that was a whole new stack of worries. Seb shouldn't have gone out on his own. He was supposed to be

185

buddying up, just like everyone else. Sure, this was a safer part of town, but not safe enough.

"I don't know," Trey said. He'd screwed up, and he deserved to be punished for it, but damn it, he didn't *want* to be punished, so he straightened to his full height and glared back at Simon. "This isn't a *jail*, you know. How the hell am I supposed to keep track of him if he sneaks off?"

"You're not," Simon said. He didn't really sound like he was accusing Trey of anything. "But he should have told you where he was going. Or he should at least pick up his phone."

Oh, so now Simon was accusing *Seb*? Hell, no. "How exactly did *you* get here? You came on your own, without safety buddies?"

"I took a cab."

"Maybe Seb took a cab, too." Probably not, since he had his own car, but maybe. "When did you start texting him? How long has it been?"

Simon looked down at his phone. "About half an hour."

Half an hour. Not long, but longer than Trey wanted to think about. If Seb was in trouble somewhere, half an hour was way too long.

But Simon didn't seem too worried about that. Instead, he was looking Trey over and apparently not liking what he saw. "It's okay that you look beat up—that's kind of the point of this. But are you *clean*? Like, are you allowed to shower? And if you're allowed to, could you please go do it?"

"I'm not supposed to get my stitches wet."

"Where are your stitches? Your face, your hand—is that it?"

"It's kinda hard to shower without getting your face or your hand wet."

"We could put a plastic bag over your hand. Your head is trickier."

Back when Trey and Seb had discussed this there'd been talk about Trey hanging his head over the tub so Seb could hand-wash his hair, but Trey wasn't going to bring that up with Simon. And it wasn't like Trey's hair was long enough to worry about. "I've been washing with a washcloth—it's not like I stink or anything. And I can try shaving…." Again, Seb had thought he'd be able to help with that, and again, Trey wasn't going to mention that to Simon. Where the hell was Seb anyway? "Text him again. Tell him to get his ass home." Because Trey needed assistance, not because he was worried. "What time are the reporters supposed to get here?"

"Just one reporter, thankfully. With a camera person." Simon pulled his phone out and said, "They could be here any minute." He tapped a message, then looked back up at Trey. "Do you have different clothes?"

"Different how?"

"Not sweat pants? How about a shirt with a collar?"

"I have jeans. But no shirts with collars, no. I don't like them around my neck."

Simon sighed. "We want you to look like a victim. Someone who got beat up, not someone who was in a fight. You know what I'm saying?"

"You're saying people who wear shirts with collars don't get in fights?"

Simon's phone buzzed and he looked down, then back up with obvious relief. "Seb's on his way. Should be here in ten minutes. And it'll take the reporter a while to get set up…." He squinted at Trey. "Show me the shirts you've got. No point trying to borrow something from Seb."

"Not if you want the shirt to cover my whole body instead of just one of my arms."

"I wonder if Shane has something?" Simon shook his head. "Probably not. Hardly ever see him in anything but a hoodie."

"I'm not wearing someone else's shirt," Trey said. "If anyone thinks I got messed up this bad in a fair fight, they can go fuck themselves. And if they're stupid enough to think the kind of shirt you wear affects whether you get in fights, they're not my problem."

"Not quite the approach we want to take in the interview," Simon said, but he gestured Trey toward the guest bedroom as if giving up on the conversation. "Show me your shirts. And then you can have a quick bath."

"A *bath*?"

"If you're lucky, I'll be able to find some bubbles for you."

Well, that was something to look forward to.

Trey left Simon poking through his meagre bag of clothes and wandered into the bathroom. A bath. Possible, he guessed. He'd had them when he was a kid. So he turned on the tap and adjusted the heat and stripped down. A moment of examination in the mirror—hardly a hand's breadth on his body that wasn't purple or fading to greenish yellow—and then a closer look at his face. A victim. That was what he was supposed to look like.

Every instinct he had screamed at him that it was a terrible idea. He needed to look strong, intimidating. He couldn't show weakness—that was giving too much away to his enemies, whoever they were.

But Simon and Tristan and Noah thought this was a good idea. *Seb* thought it was a good idea. He thought Trey could do it, and should do it. So Trey damn well would do it.

He stepped into the half-filled tub and hissed as the heat of the water washed over him. Sore muscles complained, every scratch and scrape stung like they were fresh—but that was okay. And after a few moments of adjustment, he let himself lean back and relax a little and it was more than okay. Baths were kinda good, actually. The water from the faucet kept things moving, stirring, like someone was tickling him—no, *licking* him, like a cat would lick a kitten. He was getting clean in the most gentle way possible. No complaints. And the water flowed out of the tub through the overflow drain, so he could keep the fresh water running, keep things moving, without flooding the whole bathroom.

He might have dozed off a little, or at least fallen into a bit of a trance, because before he knew it there was a gentle knock and the door opened a sliver. "Trey?" Seb's familiar voice.

"Yeah. The reporter here?"

"Not yet. Can I come in?"

Huh. Nothing Seb hadn't seen before, so Trey said, "Yeah, okay."

But when Seb stepped in and looked at him, the expression on his face made it pretty damn clear he *hadn't* seen Trey before, not since he got all bruised up.

"Baths are kinda nice," Trey said before Seb could get worked up. "And Simon wants me shaved. I don't think I can do a good job with my left hand—you said you could help me out?"

"Yeah," Seb said. "Okay. But, look, Trey—" He stopped and looked over his shoulder. "Shit, sounds like they're here. Okay. You clean enough? You want me to pour a bucket of water over your hair or anything?"

"I think I'm clean."

"Okay." Seb reached for a towel with one hand and stretched the other out to Trey. "Can you get out of there without slipping?"

Almost certainly, but Trey let Seb help him anyway, and tried not to snicker at Seb's attempt to politely avert his eyes throughout the operation. Maybe he wanted to be sure he wasn't taking advantage of the Power Imbalance.

"Where's your razor?" Seb asked once the towel was securely knotted around Trey's waist.

Trey burrowed around in the plastic bag he used to hold his few toiletries and came up with a blue plastic razor.

Seb's eyes narrowed as if Trey was holding a steaming handful of fresh shit. "No," he said flatly. "You can't use that."

Trey looked at the razor. It was fairly new, as far as he could recall. "What's the problem?"

"Jesus." Seb stalked out of the bathroom. Trey followed him as far as the bedroom, but Seb kept going and there was no way Trey was going out in front of the reporter with just a towel on. So he eased himself into the jeans and navy T-shirt Simon had set out for him, and by the time he was dressed Seb was back, shifting impatiently, a different razor in his hand.

"That one's better?" Trey asked. It definitely looked more expensive, all black and shiny silver.

"So much better," Seb said. "I wanted to throw your other one out, but I managed not to. But I'm going to really work on getting *you* to throw it out. Just so you're warned."

"If I throw out the only razor I've got, you'd better get used to seeing me with a beard. Just so *you're* warned."

"I think I'd like you with a beard," Seb said, and there was a new note in his voice. No, not new, but one Trey hadn't heard since before he'd gotten beat up. He glanced over and Seb looked back and for a moment it was just the two of them—no reporter, no camera person, no Simon—then Seb shook his head. "This is important," he said, sounding like he was reminding himself as much as Trey. "We need to get you ready. We can talk afterward."

So Trey let himself be manhandled until Seb was satisfied— they ended up with Trey sitting in a chair in front of the mirror on the bureau, Seb standing behind him and reaching around to shave Trey's face because he said it felt more natural to shave with a reflection—and then led out to meet the reporter. Belinda Mason. Trey had seen her on TV, but in person she was different. She seemed sharper, like she was smart, but also sharp like she could be kind of dangerous. Sharp like she could cut someone. Trey was glad she was on their side.

"I'd like to speak to you as well," she said to Seb. "On camera. We'll do some with just Trey, and then bring you in for a little context and background information?"

Seb looked surprised and not exactly enthusiastic, but Trey nudged him and said, "What, I'm the only one who has to do this? No way, man. You're on."

Seb nodded reluctantly. "Yeah, okay. But, damn, now *I'm* the one who needs a shave."

"There's a really good razor in my room, if you want to borrow it. You're already wearing a shirt with a collar, so that'll make Simon happy."

"Yeah?"

"Collars are peaceful. You heard it here first."

Joking with Seb stopped being quite as fun when Trey glanced over at Belinda and realized she was watching them. Watching and... what was the word? Not judging, quite. Assessing. Like she was trying to figure them out.

But Trey didn't want to be figured out, especially not by someone like her. So he pulled his game face back on, bored and tough, and didn't let his gaze follow Seb as he left the room.

"You guys are pretty close?" Belinda asked.

Trey shrugged. "He's a good guy. He's helped us out a lot."

"Very generous," she agreed. She looked at the camerawoman and said, "We ready to go?" and got a nod in return.

Trey wanted to stop them. Seb was supposed to be there, making sure everything went smoothly. Making sure Trey didn't totally fuck up. Shit, how long did it take to shave? Five minutes? Could Trey stall that long, somehow?

But he was already sitting where Belinda wanted him, and everyone else was ready. He just needed to be ready, too.

He took a deep breath and tried to smile without showing how queasy he was feeling. Questions. A beautiful, professional woman whose outfit probably cost more than every piece of clothing Trey had ever owned in his entire life. A camera, and little microphones clipped onto shirts. It was all happening, and Trey just needed to do the best he could.

He wished Seb would hurry up with the damn shaving, though.

~*~*~*~

SEB DIDN'T SHAVE. HE SPLASHED water on his face, decided his stubble was at a length that made it look deliberate rather than sloppy, and then pulled a fresh shirt out of the closet. He'd gotten dressed in a hurry that morning after a restless night; there wasn't much to do about the bags under his eyes, but at least his clothes could be un-creased.

And once the damn interview was over he'd talk to Trey, explain what he'd found, what his father had said that morning, and—he'd find a way to make it okay. Then he'd have to fix it with the larger group as well. He had some ideas for that, but he needed some time to think them through. He needed to think all of it through.

But not right then.

By the time he was back in the living room the interview had begun. Belinda had said they'd be shooting way more footage than they'd use, so that was kind of comforting; if something went terribly wrong they could just edit it out. But there was only so much of this Trey would be able to handle—he already looked like he was fighting the urge to run away—so they needed to get some good footage and be done with it.

"And you're sure the men who attacked you are connected to—to real estate development in the neighborhood?" Belinda asked. "That sounds a little far-fetched—how can you be sure it wasn't related to something else?"

"Something else?" Trey asked. He was still under control, but his shoulders were tightening and Seb's hands itched with the need to massage them back into the beautiful relaxation he'd seen in the bath.

"And what are your reasons for believing it's connected to the development?"

"They said they'd already warned me," Trey said. "And the guys who warned me were pissed that I was handing out flyers about trouble in the neighborhood. And the trouble in the neighborhood was about the real estate guys, and the fires they'd started."

"But there's no proof they started the fires, is there?" She smiled gently. "I'm not saying I don't believe you. But if someone wasn't inclined to agree with you, what arguments could we advance that would make it clear what's going on? What proof could we show them?"

Trey looked over at Seb, then for a merciful moment looked at Simon, but then was back to Seb. "I don't know about proof," he finally said. "Proof is for cops, and the cops don't seem to be too damn interested in any of this. I just know what I know."

She nodded sweetly. "Okay. So, we've gone over what happened that night—now I'd like to get a bit of context. What's been happening since then, that sort of thing."

"Since then? I was in the hospital for a few days, and I've been here for a couple days."

"And where is 'here'?"

Trey frowned at her. "You don't know where you are?"

"I do, but the audience won't. I'm not looking for an address, but can you tell us who you're staying with?"

"Uh—" He looked back to Seb. "Is it okay to say your name?"

Seb nodded. He didn't want it to happen—didn't want Trey to advertise their association on television—and he was disgusted with himself for his reticence. Like Trey was something to be ashamed of. Damn it, he needed to get rid of that attitude.

"I'm staying with Seb Tanner. He's working with us, trying to be, like, a community organizer? Like Obama was before he was president. And when I needed somewhere to stay after I got out of the hospital, he offered his spare bedroom. Just for a little while."

"That's very generous of him."

"Yeah. He's a good guy."

"And he's interested in politics? Is that why he's following in Barrack Obama's footsteps?"

"Oh. No, I don't know. I just said that because I didn't know what a community organizer was, before all this started. And when I googled it, that was what came up. Barrack Obama."

Seb hoped this part of the interview was going to get edited out. Why the hell were they talking about Obama?

"What kind of background does Seb have with community organizing?"

Jesus, was it time to step in? Trey didn't know this stuff, and he tended to get belligerent when he was uncertain. Seb looked over at Simon, who was frowning, but not speaking up. So Seb kept his mouth shut.

Trey said, "I don't know. He was working with some other guys—but they backed out when I got beat up. It was too dangerous for them, I guess, but Seb stuck around."

"And why do you think he did that?" Belinda asked, and Seb's stomach twisted in sickening realization. She wasn't asking about him as general interest; she had an angle. And there was really only one angle she could have on this, wasn't there?

He stepped forward. It was too late; the cold dread clutching his spine told him as much. But—"Can we take a quick break?" he asked. But he asked *Belinda*. He should have asked Trey. He turned his eyes in that direction but already Belinda was speaking.

"I only have another few questions for Trey, and then I'd be more than happy to interview you." She continued without even pausing for breath. "Trey, did you know that Sebastian Tanner is listed as a part owner of one of the companies that owns the real estate in question? The person you've been staying with, who's been 'helping' you through all this—did you know he's one of the people you're accusing of arranging your assault?"

Seb had thought he couldn't feel any worse, but then he saw the expression on Trey's face. Confusion, like a little kid. A frown of concentration, and then for just a second—god, so merciful that it only lasted a second, because Seb never, ever wanted to see that level of hurt again. And then—nothing. Back to the Trey he'd first met—pugnacious, stubborn, and completely closed off.

But the reaction had all been on camera, and Belinda was still focused on Trey, practically drooling with anticipation.

Seb wanted to step in. If he got closer now, if he made his excuses, explained himself... if he got any closer than he was he'd probably get punched in the face. And what excuses did he have, exactly, that Trey would believe, or even understand?

"Quick break," Seb almost gasped. And this time he directed his plea to Trey, not Belinda. "Can I just talk to you for a second?"

Trey turned dead eyes toward him. "I'm not done here," he said.

And Seb suddenly knew how it would happen. Trey knew Seb's secrets; he might not think the kink was a big deal, but he knew how Seb felt about it. Seb had hurt Trey, so now Trey would hurt Seb.

It was inevitable.

Seb didn't know the exact wording Trey would use, but that didn't really matter, did it? It was going to come out, and everyone would know. Everyone.

He grabbed hold of the back of his sofa, trying to maintain his balance. And he waited for the punishment he knew he deserved.

Instead, Trey said, "I don't know who owns what. I'm not the brains, here. You want deeper answers, you need to ask someone else."

"Yes," Belinda said patiently, "but do you understand what I've just told you? Are you concerned that you've been sharing strategies and secrets with the enemy?"

Secrets. She'd said the actual word, and surely that would trigger Trey's memory. He might have forgotten that he had the means to hurt Seb, but not anymore. He remembered now, and—

Trey turned to look at Seb and it was there in his eyes. He knew what Seb was afraid of; he'd thought of it right away. And still, he shrugged. "I got beat up for handing out flyers. You want more than that, talk to someone else."

"Yes, but—"

"Do you have any *new* questions?" Trey asked. "About stuff I can answer?" He waited a second, if that long, and then reached for the microphone on his shirt. "Okay, then, Thanks."

Every muscle in his shoulders were bulging with tension as he stood up and started moving. Three steps to where Seb was standing, then brushed by him like he wasn't there. Like he didn't exist.

"Simon can talk to you," Seb told Belinda, or at least he projected the words in her general direction; he didn't stick around to see if she'd heard him. He just didn't care.

He followed Trey with no real plan beyond the irresistible need to somehow make things better. He'd messed up, and he needed to apologize, at the very least.

Or get punched in the face. It was entirely possible that he was just going to get punched in the face.

But when he made it into Trey's bedroom and closed the door behind him, there was no assault. There wasn't even a crackle of anger. Just Trey, standing by the window and staring outside as he used to do at Tristan's.

And Seb the Charming, Seb the Glib and Smooth and Polished, stood and stared at him, and had absolutely no idea what to say.

Kate Sherwood

Chapter Eighteen

THE SILENCE WASN'T ALL THAT uncomfortable, at least for Trey. But he spoke anyway. "It wasn't your fault."

"It wasn't on purpose," Seb said. He was speaking faster than he usually did, and sounded much less confident. "I mean, it definitely wasn't on purpose that we owned those shares. Like, we weren't deliberately trying to gentrify a Seattle neighborhood or anything. My dad bought them as a good investment based on numbers and theory and whatever, without paying too much attention to details like addresses. I talked to him this morning and he explained it all, and I know that's how he invests—he bought these shares years ago and he just didn't think about them in the current context. And it wasn't on purpose that I didn't tell you—I swear. I just figured it out last night, and then there wasn't time this morning to get into it all."

"You've been digging into the financial records for days," Trey said. He wasn't arguing, really. He felt far too removed from all of this to bother to fight. He was just clarifying things in case he decided to start caring about it later, when he wasn't quite so numb. "You spent all that time on it and just found this last night?"

"It's complicated. I mean, the records are complicated. You can ask Simon—it's not like we found this and I hid it or something. We just hadn't dug back that far, yet."

Okay. Trey could let that go. He had no idea if it was true or not, but that didn't matter. "I get it."

But Seb still stood there. "I have some plans—I'm working with my dad to see who the other shareholders are—we might be able to *use* this, you know? Like, maybe we can have an emergency shareholders meeting and tell them what's going on and see if we can persuade them to back off. This could be a *good* thing, really."

A good thing. *A good thing?* Trey wasn't quite as numb as he'd thought. "I don't want them—you—I don't want anyone to *back off.* Somebody killed Jake's brother, somebody beat the shit out of me, trying to scare us so they can control what we do. *Backing off* isn't enough. I want to burn it all down."

"What's 'it', though?" Seb's voice was small again. "Do you mean... am I part of that? What about other people like me, who didn't actually know what was going on?"

Trey had no answer to that question. He had no answers to any questions, and he should have known better than to try to come up with any. The numbness was back now, the exhaustion, and the dull thudding in his head was turning into something a lot sharper and harder to ignore. He wanted to curl up in his warm, soft bed—but it wasn't *his* bed, and he'd been stupid to let himself forget that, even for a second.

"What are you doing?" Seb asked, but Trey ignored him. "Okay, yeah, you're packing. I see that. But—"

"I won't leave until the reporter's gone," Trey said. He wouldn't give her the satisfaction of knowing the damage she'd done.

"But you shouldn't leave at all! You're still recovering—the room's still available—those assholes are still out there on the streets, and once they see the interview they'll know you haven't given up." Seb sounded almost desperate. Trey should have savored that, should have felt like it was a victory. He had some power, here, after all. But it just made him even more exhausted. "Look," Seb continued, "you can make the decision, okay? I can sell the stocks—they're in trust, so I'd have to get my dad's okay, but he'd be fine with that. Or I can hold onto them and fight this from the inside. Whichever you want. Totally your call."

Jesus, Trey's head was going to explode. In slow motion, because he didn't have the energy to make a big blast. "That's not sex," he mumbled. It made sense to him, but when he forced his gaze to Seb's face he could tell he was the only one who understood. "I was in charge for sex. That's all. I don't tell you what to do the rest of the time. That's not my job."

"Couldn't it be? I mean—couldn't you at least help me?"

The scorpion asking the frog how not to sting. As if the frog would have any idea. As if the frog wasn't putting all his goddamn energy into trying to get them both across to the shore.

Trey sank down onto the bed. "Can you go away? I know, this is your place, but I can't leave yet. Unless—I guess I can, if you want me to. But I need—I need some quiet. One of us needs to go."

"You look like shit." Seb stepped closer, which really wasn't part of the plan. "Do you just need a rest, or do you need to see a doctor? Should I call my mom? Or drive you to the hospital?"

"Just a rest. I'm fine."

Trey stayed sitting up but let his eyes close. Yeah, that was better. No more pulsing lights, and no more having to look at Seb's pinched, anxious face.

"I'll go," Seb said quietly. "Just out to the kitchen, though. Not far, so if you need me—"

"I'm fine."

Trey heard the door click shut a few seconds later and let himself relax back onto the bed. Such a nice mattress. And his feet were still on the floor, so it wasn't like he was actually in bed. He was just sitting down in a bit of a strange way.

He'd taken the sting, and the venom was working its way through his body. But as long as Seb stayed away from him—as long as the frog wasn't carrying the scorpion's weight as well as his own—maybe he could keep swimming. And that was what was best for the frog, and for the scorpion as well.

~*~*~*~

"WE STILL HAVE A FEW questions we'd like to ask you, Sebastian." Belinda's smile was sweet, but her eyes were fierce. "Simon's given us some great factual content, but we're really looking more for the emotional side. Without solid proof of any of your theories, we're going to have to sell this as a human interest story if we want it to run."

Easy to translate that to 'if you don't give me what I want, I won't give you what you want.' Damn it.

"What kind of questions?" Seb asked. "What are you looking for?"

"I want the complications. The grey areas." For a moment he felt as if her hard shell dropped away and he caught a glimpse of the creature inside—hungry, ambitious, but not evil. And definitely not stupid. "*Rich bastards bully innocent poor folk* has no nuance. I want some depth, some—well, some human interest, in the true meaning of the phrase."

"And you're willing to ambush people and ruin relationships in order to get it."

"If the relationship is ruined by simple truths, possibly it wasn't that strong to begin with."

Seb wanted to throw her out. It had been a mistake to let the world into his apartment, and he should have known better. This was his sanctuary, the one place he'd been able to be honest about who he was and what he wanted, and now? It had been defiled.

Or—oh, god, was he brave enough? Not for anything about the kind of sex he liked; that wasn't a question of lying, it was just nobody else's business. But could he be honest about everything else? Knowing his family would watch, his friends, strangers he didn't know but would someday meet… could he actually let himself be honest with this woman, with this woman's *camera*, knowing who might see it?

He thought of Trey, who couldn't stand to be in the same room with Seb anymore. Trey wasn't going to listen to Seb, not anytime soon. But maybe, just maybe, he'd listen to this woman's broadcast. Maybe he'd stop looking so worn out, so disappointed, if he could just understand that Seb was as lost as everyone else. Maybe.

"We can introduce you to some other members of the team," Simon said to Belinda, but she barely acknowledged that he had spoken. She kept her gaze locked on Seb, as if she could read his mind and knew how close he was to giving her what she wanted.

"I can give you a copy of the footage," she said. "I can't make any promises about what I'll actually air, but if you just want a record, I can help you with that."

"Okay," he said. A record sounded pretty good. Trey wouldn't listen to it right away, but someday, he might. And that would have to be enough for Seb.

He crossed the room and let them attach the mike to his shirt. Simon was in the background, on the phone, and Seb hoped he was calling Tristan. Seb had been the Trey-wrangler for a while, but he wasn't sure the honor was going to be continued, and Trey was not yet in any condition to look after himself. If Tristan could get over here, he could step in and make sure Trey was safe. That was the number one priority. Seb would worry about everything else later.

~*~*~*~

TREY WOKE UP SLOWLY and took a moment to figure out where the hell he was. Warm, comfortable, everything good—oh. His memory kicked him hard.

For a brief, tantalizing moment he thought about forgetting it all. He could unpack his stuff, go out to the other room and bitch at Seb about something soup-related, and just let it go. Did it matter, really? So Seb owned some stocks or something... was it that big of a deal?

But if it wasn't a big deal for Seb, did that mean it wasn't a big deal for anyone else either? All of the people they'd been trying to track down and confront should be allowed to just walk away from what had been done in their name? It didn't matter if people were getting hurt so you could make more money as long as you didn't have personal knowledge of what was happening?

The assholes who'd killed Jake's brother, who'd beat Trey up—they were the only ones who should be blamed. Don't bother asking who hired them, or why. There's nothing wrong with the system—this was just a little glitch. Sit back and relax. Everything's fine.

Trey heaved himself upright, ignoring the now-familiar agony in his ribs. There was a middle ground. Trey didn't have to hate Seb, but he couldn't let himself ignore it all, either.

He scooped his backpack off the foot of the bed and looked around the room for anything he'd left behind. It looked lived-in, but Seb had already mentioned that he had a cleaning service that came in once a week; they'd take care of the sheets or whatever. Just one more mess Seb didn't have to take care of himself.

Good, yeah, stick to that. Get pissed at him. That'll make everything way easier.

Trey opened the bedroom door cautiously and snuck a look down the hall. He couldn't see far enough to be sure the coast was clear, so he listened, and heard nothing. The reporter must be gone; she wasn't the sort to just sit somewhere quietly, was she?

No, he realized after he made it to the end of the hall, *she* wasn't that sort, but Tristan was. Flopped down on Seb's million-dollar leather couch like it was totally natural for him to be there, apparently all alone, just—waiting. For what?

"Where's Seb?" Trey asked as soon as Tristan looked up.

"He went out. He said you'd wanted some space." He held up his cell. "He said he'd stay in the neighborhood and I should call him if you wanted to talk."

Jesus. Trey had pushed the guy out of his own home. "I don't want to talk. Why are you here?"

Tristan sighed. "He said you were thinking about leaving. So I'm here to make sure you don't do anything stupid. Jake drove me over and he'll come pick us up if we want; you can come stay at my place if you don't want to be here."

"*If* I don't want to be here? You heard about all this, right? You know that Seb's one of the guys we were trying to track down? He says he didn't know about it—"

"And Simon's confirmed that it's totally possible he didn't know. They hadn't come across the company name yet, and it doesn't sound like Seb ever took an active role in running his finances."

"Because he has people to take care of that for him. People with money don't have to get their own hands dirty. They don't have to feel guilty about what they do because they're so far removed from it all. But all this shit that's happened? It's happened because of Seb and people like him."

Tristan raised an eyebrow. "So that's a *yes* on you not wanting to stay here?"

"We're not all whores, you know. Money doesn't buy everybody."

But Tristan didn't rise to the bait, didn't give Trey the fight he wanted. "Is that all your stuff? Should I give Jake a call, or do you think we'd be okay on the bus?"

The bus. Back to Tristan's couch, or sleeping rough, or slumming around in the shelters. Back to Trey's old life. No more soft bed, no more baths, no more mom-soup. But Trey could do without all of that.

No more Seb.

That was what was really going to hurt. But it had been inevitable. Trey was tired of thinking about scorpions and frogs and rivers, but that didn't mean he could afford to let go of the message. Trey should have known better than to have let himself get comfortable. Should have known better than to think he could be friends—could be something *more* than friends—with someone whose life was so totally different from his own.

"The bus is fine," he mumbled.

Tristan stood up. "So you're ready to go?"

It felt wrong to leave without saying goodbye. Stupid, but true. Trey wanted to leave a note, but he had no idea what he could possibly write that would make any sense. He had enough trouble just speaking words; he sure as hell didn't need to start messing around with writing them.

"The interview was pretty much a disaster," he told Tristan as they headed for the door.

"Simon said there was enough good stuff that she could make it work if she wants to."

"He must have given her most of that himself, then. My part sucked." He hit the button for the elevator.

"Seb spoke to her too. Simon said—well, he seemed to think it could be useful."

Useful. Trey was so tired of trying to figure out what might be *useful*. Why couldn't things just *be*? Why couldn't he just sit on the couch and have Seb bring him soup, and why couldn't his ribs stop hurting every time he moved, because after the soup it would be really nice to see Seb on his knees, looking up at Trey with that crazy mix of defiance and submission and fucking *hunger*....

Shit. No. That was over. It had barely even been started, and it was gone. They stepped onto the elevator and rode it down in silence, then started walking to the bus stop.

"So what if the interview *is* useful?" Trey asked. No, he didn't want to think about it, but it was better than the alternatives. Boring was better than painful. "What's the next step?"

"Still the rally—protest—we're working out the exact wording. It'll be better if the interview airs because we'll get more supporters and hopefully more attention, but we're going to go ahead with it either way."

"And what are we hoping for?" It was a question that probably had a different answer now than it had a few hours earlier. "How do we win this? Like, what do we even want?"

For the first time Trey noticed how tired Tristan looked. Like everyone was kind of shook up about this new situation, and kind of worried about it. But he still sounded like calm old Tristan when he said, "We should have a meeting, I think. One without Seb there. We need to decide—he told me he still wants to be part of this, if we'll let him. He had some ideas about how to actually use his shares to help us. But—I don't know."

"You think you can ask Jake and Micah to sit in the same room with him?"

"I can ask. But I sure as hell can't criticize them if they say no." Tristan paused, then added, "What about you? You're a victim here, too. Simon said the cops are thinking about this as attempted murder, not just aggravated assault." They reached the bus stop and Tristan turned toward Trey. It was harder to lie face-to-face, and Tristan knew it. "I know you don't want to stay at his place anymore, but are you okay if we keep working with him? Are you okay spending time with him?"

"I don't know." Trey felt like a little kid—a *stupid* little kid who couldn't even figure out how he felt about something totally basic. "I—I'm not mad at him. I don't blame him. But—" *But it hurts to look at him or think about him. I let myself get dragged in even though I knew better all along and it's humiliating to have to admit how dumb I was. It's only been a couple hours since I saw him and already I miss him like my arm got cut off.* "He has good soup."

And Tristan, bless his heart, nodded as if that was a reasonable answer. "We could make that a condition of his involvement. We could say he has to be our caterer."

"I don't think he makes the soup himself. His mom does." And that should be another reason to resent him, of course. It wasn't Seb who'd put the effort into looking after Trey, it was his mother. And she hadn't made it because she wanted to feed people who needed feeding; Seb said she made soup when she was stressed. She made it to help herself, not anyone else. It was nothing for Trey to feel grateful about. Just one more perk from being born Sebastian Tanner.

"Maybe it's time he learned to make his own soup," Tristan said.

The bus came then, and they climbed on board and sat without speaking. Stares from other passengers reminded Trey that his face was still battered, and it was strange to realize how quickly everything was happening. He'd only known Seb for a week and a half, only spent four or five nights at his place. One fuck, one blowjob, and some soup.

It was nothing.

Nothing.

Trey slouched down in his seat and let his eyes close. It had all been nothing, and it hadn't really affected him. He'd been fine before, and he'd be fine after. It wasn't a big deal. "I don't care," he said without opening his eyes. "If Seb's still part of it. Whatever. If you guys think you can use him, it doesn't matter to me."

It doesn't matter. It doesn't matter. Trey repeated the words to himself, matched them up with the dull, throbbing pain in his head. *It doesn't matter. It doesn't matter. Nothing matters.*

He'd always been able to convince himself before, and he'd damn well convince himself again. He just needed a little time. Time, and some way to get Seb Tanner the hell out of his head.

Chapter Nineteen

SEB HADN'T WANTED TO GO back to his apartment. He'd known it would feel empty without Trey, and when he finally forced himself inside, it felt just as awful as he'd known it would.

He thought about going back out. He could call Brock and see if he wanted to go for a beer; hell, even nasty craft beer was better than being in the apartment alone.

But Brock knew Seb too well; he'd see something was wrong, and he'd want to know what it was, and Seb just wasn't up to talking about any of it.

Still, when Allison called a little after six, he picked up the phone. And it was kind of gratifying to hear her sounding genuinely upset as she said, "Dad told me. He feels terrible, and now *I* feel terrible. We had the stupid ethical filters for it all—no tobacco, no weapons, no tar sands—but we didn't go deep enough. And I *asked* him to look for things closer to home! I said I'd rather own shares in Seattle real estate than in some buildings in France or whatever. God, Seb, this is partly my fault!"

"The buildings in France might be screwing over the locals, too."

"But the locals wouldn't be people you were working with! Have you told them? Are they taking it okay?"

"I don't really know." That was true. Trey had seemed so—empty. So absent. All the intensity that made him so exciting to be around had just vanished. So that didn't seem like taking it *well*. But he hadn't punched Seb in the face, either. "I think they're still thinking it through."

"I told Dad I'd totally support whatever you want to do. If you say we should sell, we'll sell. No problem. Or if you want to try to do some stockholder activism stuff, I'm with you. We could ask Dad to buy *more* shares, even, to give us more of a voice."

"I'm not sure we should have more of a voice." As he spoke the words, they seemed to crystalize some realization that had been creeping in from the edges of his thoughts. "Isn't the problem that we've already got way too big of a voice? Like, isn't part of the point of all this that *other* people should have a voice?"

"So what are you suggesting? We should—what? How do we make it better?"

"Maybe we don't." It wasn't what he wanted to say, wasn't what he wanted to *think*, but he couldn't let that matter. "Maybe this time we just stay out of the way, and let somebody *else* make it better."

"The people you've been working with? You think they actually have a chance of getting something done, on their own?"

"I think—yeah, actually, I think they do. I mean, it might not work, but—" He struggled to find the words. He hadn't wanted to talk about this, and still didn't want to talk about the Trey part of it all, but the rest? He needed to figure it out, and Allison might be able to help. "It's not that important that the neighborhood not get gentrified. I mean, it *is*—the people who live there don't have anywhere else to go, so if rents start going through the roof they're going to be kind of screwed, but—I don't know. These people are used to being kind of screwed, you know? They'd probably just have rolled over and taken it if it was just that." He was on the right track; he could feel it. He could hear Trey's voice—*'Backing off isn't enough. I want to burn it all down.'* "This is about something bigger. The fires, the beatings—that's not just capitalism being insensitive to people without money. You know? It's bullying, it's fucking *murder*, and I've been talking up the cops and saying they're doing their best, but I'm really not sure they are. I'm really not sure anybody's ever going to be punished for those crimes."

He paused and tried to re-organize his thoughts. "So if we sell our stocks, or if we buy more stocks and keep the neighborhood from getting gentrified—the first one keeps our hands clean, but doesn't do any more. And the second, assuming it worked, would only solve part of the problem. And not the big part. The big part of the problem is that people with money—people like you and me, Al—thought they could get what they wanted by playing rough. And they thought they could get away with it because nobody cares what happens to some junkies and some street kids."

"But somebody *does* care," Allison said softly.

"Yeah. I care. But that's not the important part. The important part is that *they* care. They're standing up for themselves and they're getting organized and they're drawing a fucking line in the sand and saying 'no more'. It's *them*, Al. That's what's important about this."

She didn't answer right away. After a while, though, she said, "So what do we do? You and me? You more than me, obviously, but—I'll follow your lead."

"I don't think I'm going to be doing any leading, not on this one."

"The stocks, though. You want to just leave them? You want to collect some nice dividends that were only earned because somebody got *killed*?"

"Yeah. I mean, no, obviously I don't *want* that. And I'll donate any dividends from the stocks to some relevant cause, just to do that tiny bit to ease my guilt. But—I don't think we should sell. It's too late, isn't it?" Too late for Jake's brother, too late for Trey. "The damage has been done. Selling now would—I don't know. The problem would still be there. We'd just be—I don't know how to explain it. And obviously whatever I'm trying to say, whatever I'm trying to do, it could all change if he—if *they* want it to. If they all decide we should sell, or if they want us to try to use our shares, then I think we should do what they want. But if they leave it up to us?"

"We should take the hit," she said softly. "We should recognize that we can talk a good game about social responsibility but that doesn't mean too much when we're living the way we live and other people are living the way *they* live, all because we were lucky enough to be born into a certain family."

"Yeah," he said. "Something like that."

"I don't like it, baby brother. I prefer my liberal guilt to be a little less concrete, a little more removed. But I guess that's kind of the point you're making, right?"

"I think so. Or, shit, I don't know, maybe I'm just making everything more difficult than it has to be."

"People have died. I'd say it's time things started being difficult."

"We're not bad people." Seb wasn't sure if he'd have been as confident if he was just saying it about himself, but when he added in Allison and his parents it was easier to be compassionate. "We don't want to hurt anyone, and none of this was deliberate. We didn't mean for it to happen. But we're part of the system. And the system apparently makes some people think it's okay to bully and murder poor people. The system seems to be letting them get away with it."

"So what are you saying? You want to be a revolutionary? You want to tear it all down?"

Tear it, burn it—there wasn't much difference. "No, I don't want to do that. But I understand why other people do. And I—I don't think I should get in their way."

"Seb—" She was clearly searching for the right words. "Be careful, okay? I mean, physically careful, obviously. I know Mom and Dad have already been all over you about that. But it's not just physical. Right?"

For a moment he thought she meant it wasn't just *sex*, and it was strange to think she'd been able to put that into words before he had. But then he realized she was still talking about the danger. Not just physical danger.

"I guess not," he admitted.

"No guessing about it. If this guy—I mean, these people—I hear what you're saying about them having good reason to be angry. I agree with you. But if you trust him—them—oh, fuck it. Seb, if you trust *him*, and he hurts you because he's angry about your economic privilege? Just because you understand it doesn't mean it's going to hurt any less. Do you know what I'm saying?"

Seb swallowed hard. "Yeah. I know."

"So you're going to be careful? I'm not saying you shouldn't care, but—damn. Don't care *too much*, you know?"

It was too late for that, he realized. His sister was giving him good advice, but she should have shared it a couple weeks ago.

Of course, back then he wouldn't have listened to her. He'd been so sure of himself, so confident that he had it all figured out. He'd known who he was and what he cared about and the only thing that had shaken him, even a little—he thought of Trey laughing at him, teasing him about his *fetish*—he'd stopped worrying about, and started worrying about every other damn thing.

"Seb?" Allison said. "You still there?"

"Yeah. Sorry. I—it's not easy to know how much is too much, is it?"

"In terms of caring? No, I guess it isn't. And I know you can't go through life in totally defensive mode all the time. But—I don't know. I'm your older sister. It's my job to worry about you, right?"

"And my job to worry about you?"

"Sure, yeah, when I need it. But right now, I'm fine. So let's focus on you."

It was shocking to feel the pressure behind his eyes, to realize how close he was to crying. Because his sister cared about him? Seriously?

But, yeah. Because a solid, affectionate family was just one more gift Seb had taken for granted all his life, one more way his situation was so much easier than Trey's. "I love you, Al. I don't like dark beer and I'm not going to drink it anymore. But I love you."

"I—okay. What? Why are you talking about beer all of a sudden?"

Because he'd been overcome by a powerful urge to share secrets, and it was a hell of a lot better to tell her about beer than to tell her he liked guys to push him around when they had sex. "I just thought you should know."

"If you start giving away your possessions, I'm calling Mom and Dad."

"I'm not giving my possessions away. If I gave away my fridge, I'd have nowhere to keep my cheap-ass, so-pale-it-might-as-well-be-water beer. That I like."

"How many times have I seen you drinking dark beer?"

"Many, many times. But not anymore."

"How many times have I *served* you dark beer when you came to my house?"

"A lot."

"But those days are over."

"You can still serve it to me if you want. But I probably won't drink it." And that seemed like a metaphor, somehow. Something about not being able to control other people, but at least taking responsibility for himself. Seb wished Trey were there so he could try to talk it through with him. Trey would be grumpy and pretend not to understand, but he'd listen, and... shit. That wasn't how things were going to be anymore.

"Is there a preferred variety of donkey-piss I should keep in stock for when you visit?"

He shouldn't have been tempted to cry again, not just because his sister was a good host. Damn, his emotions were out of control. "Any donkey you can find is good by me."

"Okay." Her voice was a little softer now, and he braced himself. "And you'll come over if you need someone to talk to, or someone to hang out with, okay? We can just watch TV or something if you want."

"And eat ice cream out of the carton?"

"If it comes to that, I'll be prepared."

"Thanks, Al."

"Keep me in the loop about the stocks. If there's anything we should be doing, we'll do it. Clear?"

"Yeah," he said. Then she hung up and he was alone again.

Kate Sherwood

Chapter Twenty

TREY DIDN'T ARGUE TOO HARD when everyone insisted he move back onto Tristan's couch. He was still bruised and battered and feeling like shit, and while the couch might be uncomfortable compared to the bed in Seb's guest room, it was a hell of a lot comfier than the ground.

And more importantly, he didn't want to be alone. Stupid, but true. Being distracted, even annoyed, by the constant activity at Tristan's was a hell of a lot better than being somewhere quiet where he might actually have time to think about things he'd rather forget.

So he spent the night on the couch. Broken ribs made it hard to be comfortable anywhere, much less on a lumpy and too-short sofa, so he had a good excuse for not sleeping well. And not sleeping well was a good excuse for his reaction the next morning when Tristan told him Seb had called and wanted to come over, if that was okay with everybody.

Yeah, it was just because he hadn't gotten a good night's sleep. It made him light-headed or something, and that was why he

225

felt the flash of excitement, of *anticipation* at the thought of seeing Seb. And it was also why it hit so damn hard when he remembered that Seb was—not the enemy, exactly. But one of *them*. One of the wealthy overclass who lived their golden lives in the clouds. Not someone Trey could—no, of course he wasn't someone Trey could have ever, like—no. But not even someone he could be friends with, really. He'd known he was being stupid as he was doing it, so he had no one to blame but himself.

He was standing at his old spot by the window, looking out at the street, when Seb's SUV pulled up to the curb. Nothing happened for quite a while after the car stopped, but eventually the driver's door opened, Seb climbed out, looked up at the window— and froze. Finally he raised one hand, just barely above his waist, probably the most cautious greeting Trey had ever seen in his life. Trey raised his own hand in return, and Seb nodded before kicking himself into gear and heading toward the door.

So that was how they were going to play it. Careful, but peaceful. A truce.

Fair enough.

"Seb's coming up," Trey said without turning around. Most of the gang was there; only Noah was missing, because he had a class and Shane had practically flipped out at the idea that he might want to skip it.

So Seb was walking into a pretty loaded situation. And it was absolutely pathetic that Trey wanted to do something to protect him. Wanted to tell the others to be nice. As if Seb couldn't take care of himself. As if there was any reason for him to give half a shit whether a bunch of punks in some raggedy apartment approved of him or not.

But he did look nervous when he walked in. Like a kid called to the principal's office. But Seb had probably had a *headmaster* or some private school shit like that. Whatever—he looked like he knew he was going to get yelled at.

Or just *glared at*, maybe.

Seb took it well, at least on the outside. He shook hands with Tristan and murmured a few words that were too quiet for Trey to hear, then turned and found Jake. A few steps forward, and then, "I'm sorry. I didn't know I was part of this, but I was. I have to take responsibility for at least some of what's happened. For your brother—Austin. I'm sorry for being part of what they did to him."

Jake didn't answer right away, and he didn't hold out his hand to be shaken, but he nodded, at least. He'd heard what had been said; that was something. And he wasn't throwing punches, so that was more of something.

Seb turned to look at the others. A quick sweep of his eyes over the small crowd, not landing anywhere, barely focusing—not acknowledging Trey at all.

Because why would he? That was fine. It was done. All over.

"I'm truly grateful that you guys let me come over," Seb said. He sounded smooth, but not *too* smooth. More genuine than he had that first day, making his little speech after the other suit had introduced him. "I can totally understand if you feel betrayed, or

227

feel like I don't have a role to play anymore. But I wanted to make it clear, in case it mattered to anyone, that I'll handle this however you want. If you think it's best that I sell the shares, I'll sell them, and I'll make it clear to everyone *why* I'm selling them. Or if you want me to try to buy more—I don't know if I could buy enough to make a difference—my parents are well-off, but I don't actually have that much money myself—but if you want me to try that, I'll try it. If you want me to go away and leave you alone—I mean, if that's what everyone wants, that's what I'll do. You guys are in charge of this, okay?"

It was a strange echo of earlier conversations about who had what power and when, and Trey wondered if it meant anything, if it tied into the deal he and Seb had made—but of course that deal was over with, so how could this be anything but a coincidence?

The rest of the gang was standing awkwardly, frowning at Seb, sending furtive glances toward Jake, toward Trey—looking for reactions.

So, fine. Trey could give them at least something.

"I don't know about the stocks," he said. "That's for Simon or whoever to figure out—it's a strategy thing, right? I can't say anything about that. But the sticking-around-or-leaving part?" He shrugged, and it only hurt a little. "The demonstration is in two days and we still have a fuck-ton of work to get done. Flyers and all the rest of it. Talking to people, making sure everyone knows what's going on. We need someone who can talk to the fancy people. More than just Simon, right? So—I say we can't afford to be turning help away."

"Yeah, if we *trusted* him," Becky said, her tone making it clear that she didn't.

"He may be useful even if we don't," Simon said. He looked at Seb, maybe as an apology, maybe as something else. "We don't really have any secrets; our strategy is pretty obvious to anyone who's paying attention. So there's no harm in having him around. If we can use him as a spokesperson, at least for some groups, that's potentially useful. And—" Another hard-to-read look in Seb's direction—"there's some advantage to the idea of a human shield. We already know that no one cares if any of *us* get hurt. But if something happened to him, it'd be a hell of a stink. We have to assume that our enemy has thought of that. So having him around is a kind of protection for the rest of us."

"Like a hostage." Becky sounded pretty satisfied with that idea.

"That's fair," Seb said quickly. "That's a good idea."

No, it wasn't. They shouldn't be using Seb as a shield, they should be *shielding* him. *Trey* should be shielding him. But he managed to keep himself from saying so, even though he had to clench his jaw shut hard enough to send shocks of pain out from his broken cheekbone.

"Anyone object?" Tristan asked. "I'd say you could argue against him being included on the team at all—if you want to do that, now's the time to do it. If you'd just rather not work with him yourself, you can say so now, or you can let me know later."

So Trey didn't have to do it. He couldn't use necessity as an excuse for his actions. Except it really *was* necessary. Not that he do it publicly, but that he do it, and he couldn't trust himself not to back out if he left it for later. So he nodded at Tristan and said, "The second one. For me."

And then he didn't look at Seb again for the rest of the meeting.

~*~*~*~

IT FELT LIKE SEB HAD travelled back in time to when this had all started and nobody had trusted him or wanted him around. But it had been easier back then because he'd had his own self-confidence, his arrogant assumption that he was right and they were wrong and sooner or later they'd accept him. They'd realize they liked him. Everyone liked Seb Tanner, after all.

Yeah, right.

He tried to think of it as another gut check moment. Another time when Seb had to decide what sort of person he wanted to be, and then follow through. He wanted to be someone who stuck it out when things got rough, someone who stood by people even if they *weren't* feeding his ego and admiring him. He wanted to be the kind of person Trey would respect in the abstract, even if Trey didn't want anything to do with him in reality.

So he stuck it out. He worked with Simon, mostly, and when the time came he pulled on his dress shirt and pressed trousers and tried to get meetings with local politicians, police officials, media types—anyone who might be useful. When he actually got a few minutes of anyone's time he used all his traditional charm and mixed it with true passion, and it generally seemed as if people were listening to him. Or else they were just as smooth as he'd always been, just as good at seeming interested even when they were thinking about something totally different.

Two days of hard work, two nights of restless sleep in his too-empty apartment. He thought briefly about inviting some company over, somebody to push him or punish him, someone who could take his mind off everything else. But he didn't want a random stranger.

The local television station aired the interview the night before the protest, and he forced himself to watch. Belinda Mason was all gentle smiles and sad eyes as she introduced the story.

It took about five words for him to realize she hadn't been joking when she said she was going to present it as a human interest story, not a socio-political issue. There was a shot of Trey starting on the relatively unbruised side of his face and then scanning over to his bruised, battered cheekbone; a shot of Seb looking painfully preppy and earnest; and then a voiceover from Simon saying "They weren't looking for trouble. They just got in the way of the wrong people."

He'd probably been talking about the junkies who'd died in the fire, but that wasn't the spin Belinda was taking. She ran through the facts of it all, sure, but just a quick gloss, and then her big reveal, and Seb had to watch Trey react again to the bombshell she dropped. He wanted to turn off the television. Leave the room, or the country. But he forced himself to sit there. He'd hurt Trey, and he wouldn't let himself pretend it hadn't happened.

Then it was him and Belinda. He couldn't actually remember what he'd said; he knew he'd wanted to make things better, to be honest, but everything had been a blur. Had he managed to get any of that across? And if he had? Shit.

Trey had made it crystal clear he didn't want to have anything to do with Seb. So if Seb had managed to get his feelings across, would it make things any better? Or would it actually be worse?

TREY WANTED TO TURN THE TV off. Leave the room. Leave town. He definitely didn't want to sit there with everyone else listening spellbound as he'd grunted out whatever stupid crap he'd said to the damn reporter.

But standing up would call even more attention to himself so he stayed still, stared at the screen, and waited for it to be over.

Then Seb's face appeared. He looked—shit, it shouldn't matter how he looked, but when he had that strained, miserable expression, it damn well did. Trey wanted to—and, again, it shouldn't matter what Trey wanted to do. He needed to smarten up and stop caring about things that were out of his reach.

Still, he couldn't keep himself from listening. So he heard it when Seb said, "I came into this so full of myself. I thought I knew everything, understood everything. I thought I was—" He stopped and frowned as if he was trying to decide how much to share. Then he shrugged, not casually, but as if he was just sort of giving up. "I thought I was better than them. Better than the people I was trying to help. I thought that me working for a community group was some sort of sign of moral superiority. But it's not like I was *sacrificing* anything to work there. It wasn't a totally glamorous job, maybe, but big deal." He looked at—well, at the camera, but it *felt* like he was looking right at Trey. "But other people were volunteering their time, risking their safety—their lives, even. Trey could have been killed. He's a good guy, a great friend, totally focussed on protecting everyone else, like he thinks—like he thinks it *doesn't matter* if he gets hurt. But it matters to me. And it matters to his friends. And it's totally messed up that he thinks otherwise, and the fact that he was able to grow up thinking that? In a society as rich as ours, in clean, beautiful Seattle—that's a problem."

He took a deep breath and Trey leaned forward a little. When Seb spoke again, his usual polish was back, but his voice was even stronger than usual, even more compelling. "The developers trying to move into the neighborhood, and the tactics they're using? That's just a symptom of the larger problem. People with money acting like other people don't matter? Like they can just be rolled over? That's the big issue. It's something I've been guilty of—not consciously, but that doesn't really matter, right?"

"So what's next?" Belinda prompted. "You sound like you've got a real passion for this—have you considered politics?"

Seb frowned, although Trey couldn't see why. Seb would be a good politician, one who could actually convince Trey to take the trouble of voting.

"I'm not someone who should be leading this fight," Seb finally said. "I should be following. I have way too much to learn about everything, including myself. And this isn't—" Another frown, and then a smile, one that made Trey's ribs ache. "This isn't about me," Seb said as if it were a revelation. A blessing. "For this, *I'm* the one who doesn't matter. Trey does. Everyone else does. But me? I need to be a follower for a while." Then he looked right at the camera again, right at Trey. "I need to let other people be in charge."

"And what about Trey?" Belinda's voice was too gentle, too sweet to be trusted.

But Seb barely seemed to notice her. "I don't know if he'll trust me again," he told the camera. "If he does, it will be—a gift. If he doesn't, I can't blame him. But—whatever happens with him, it doesn't affect what I've decided for *me*, if that makes sense. I need to change. I need to wake up and understand how all of this truly works, not just how it works in my safe little world. I'm going to do that. I'm determined. If I do it on my own, that's—

that's okay. If Trey's willing to help me out? That'd be—it'd be great."

And then it was back to Belinda in the studio, and through the buzzing in his brain Trey heard her mention the protest the next day, so that was good, he supposed. But he wasn't paying much attention to that anymore.

He pushed himself to his feet, ignoring his body's complaints.

"You can't go anywhere on your own," Tristan said at the same time as Jake's "I can drive you if you want to go over there."

Trey frowned at them. "The roof. I'm going up to the roof."

"Oh." Tristan sounded strangely disappointed.

So Tristan was getting sick of having Trey on his couch. After the protest things would settle down and Trey could go back to his old sleeping habits.

Because that was what had to happen, he reminded himself as he headed up the stairs to the roof. He had to go back to normal. He had to forget things had ever been different. Some pretty words on a TV show didn't change reality. Seb felt guilty. Fair enough, maybe he *should* feel that way. Not for being part of getting Trey hurt—he hadn't been part of that, not really. But for the way everything was easy for him.

Except—shit. Trey didn't want Seb to feel guilty. Not for any of it. He wanted Seb to be happy and laughing and confident and golden. And he wouldn't be that way if he was hanging around Trey, having to look after him all the time and being reminded of how different they were.

235

So Trey stood on the roof and looked up at the clouds and imagined the stars that were behind them. He let himself think about his sisters, just a little bit. Then he clumped back down the stairs. It was annoying to be in a big crowd down in the apartment, but it was better than being alone.

Chapter Twenty-one

IT WAS STRANGE TO HAVE Brock sitting on Seb's couch. He'd visited the apartment when Seb had first moved in, tried to invite himself over a few times since, and then apparently realized that he wasn't welcome. But he'd shown up that morning, casual and unannounced, carrying enough gear to see him through the Siege of Leningrad. Apparently he'd decided to accompany Seb to the protest.

Now he brandished a kitchen spray bottle for Seb's approval. "It's equal parts Maalox and water. I made one for you, too, in case we get separated."

"Maalox?" Seb asked. "What's Maalox for?"

"Heartburn, normally. But in this format?" He lifted the spray bottle. "We can use it to rinse our faces if we get sprayed with tear gas or whatever."

"Jesus, we're not going to get tear-gassed."

"You're sure about that?"

"It's a legal protest. We've got permits and everything."

"Still, you never know," Brock said.

237

"Are you sure you want to be part of this, then? I mean—you don't have to be. I didn't expect you to be." He hadn't mentioned the protest to any of his friends or family, after all.

"I know, you didn't think we'd want to be involved. And that's not exactly flattering. You think you're all 'woke' and progressive, but the rest of us are just continuing with our shallow bourgeois lives? You think you're the only one who cares about poverty issues or whatever?"

"*Or whatever?*"

Brock waved a dismissive hand. "Yeah, I knew I shouldn't have said that as soon as it was out of my mouth. Let it go. Focus on the part where you deliberately excluded me from this important event in your life." He looked marginally more serious when he added, "Sometimes it feels like you're excluding me from a *lot* of your life." Then he smiled. "If you want to get rid of me, though, you're going to have to be a lot less subtle. I'm not very good at taking hints."

"I don't want to get rid of you." Surprising to realize how true the statement was. Even having Brock in the apartment was— okay. Strange, but okay. "I take you for granted, maybe—I just assume you'll always be there. I *like* that you'll always be there. So if you're thinking that you need to get tear-gassed as some sort of grand declaration—"

"I don't *need* to get tear-gassed. But if I do get tear-gassed, I *need* to be prepared." Brock pressed his extra spray bottle into Seb's hand. "And so do you."

"Does this stuff actually work?"

"No idea. Probably not—I mean, it'd be pretty sad for all the evil scientists who spent years of their lives perfecting tear gas if there's a totally effective, cheap, and easy antidote available at every drugstore."

"Maybe not evil," Seb tried. "Maybe just—misdirected."

Brock made a face that was likely meant to be sympathetic. "Allison told me about the Allistian thing. Sucks."

There wasn't much more to say to that, so Seb just headed for the door, and Brock trailed along after him.

"I'll drive," Brock said as they started down the stairs. "I brought the dog car."

The fur-imbued station wagon Brock's family used whenever they were bringing their two Bernese Mountain Dogs along. "You think we might adopt a pet?"

"It's our oldest car. Nobody's going to worry if it gets banged up a little."

"We're not visiting a war zone, you know."

Brock actually stopped walking. "Do you watch the news, Seb? I mean—if this is some conscious effort, some we-can't-normalize-violence sociopolitical statement you're making, then, okay, that's one thing. But if you're honestly unaware of the possibility that this event could go bad, given the current climate... the things that have happened at other protests... the fact that there's already been significant violence around this situation already...."

"It's just a little march," Seb said. He'd stood still while Brock was speaking, but he started walking again now. "Broad daylight, police presence, *Seattle*."

"Seattle isn't magic," Brock grumbled. "Bad shit can happen here. It already has."

"At night. In the dark."

"Your friend got beat up in broad daylight."

"He was alone. We won't be alone."

"You're an optimist." They were outside now and Brock jerked his head down the street. "We're down there."

Seb turned in the indicated direction, then turned back. "We. You didn't tell me there was a 'we'. I mean—"

"Did I forget to mention them?" Brock smiled.

Seb's parents. His sister and her husband. Several friends from school. All standing expectantly around the dog car and an old Range Rover.

"They can't all come," Seb said. "It could be dangerous."

"Nope. Not in Seattle, in the daytime, etcetera."

"But—"

"But nothing." They were still far enough away that the group wouldn't be able to hear them, and Brock stopped walking again. "Don't be a dick about this, Seb. These people are here to support you. I mean, they care about the cause, I'm sure, but mostly? You. Whatever's gotten up your ass in the last couple years, whatever's made you pull away from people who care about you? Let it go, at least for today. Let them care. Okay?"

Seb swallowed hard. People had thought he was pulling away? Or, more accurately, they'd *realized* he was pulling away? And they'd cared.

Brock was the one to start walking this time. "Also," he said over his shoulder, "stop drinking dark beer if you don't like it. Have a fucking white wine spritzer if you want. Nobody gives a shit."

It was a little too close to the way Trey had laughed about Seb's deep, dark secret. *Nobody gives a shit.* Not about the secrets, the weirdnesses, the ways Seb was different. Everybody else was fine with it.

Alternatively, Seb was making too big of a deal about a damn beverage choice. It wasn't like he'd shown up for a family dinner with a collar around his neck and an aggressive Dom at the other end of the leash.

And it wasn't like he ever would, he realized. It was okay for him to keep some stuff to himself. Private wasn't the same as secret, and secret wasn't the same as shameful. "I also don't like those sushi burritos your mom served last month. I don't care if they're trendy—they were gross."

"I'll be sure to let her know."

"Dark chocolate is bullshit."

"Dark chocolate *and* dark beer—possibly you're developing a pattern of being bitter about bitter flavors."

"The burritos weren't bitter. They were just too much raw fish for one damn mouthful."

And then they were at the cars, thankfully, and Seb was drawn into the wave of happy greetings and plan making and general—general belonging. He was with his people, and they were with him.

There was someone missing, of course. But Seb would see Trey soon, and maybe, just maybe, Trey would have forgiven him. Maybe he'd give Seb a chance to see if there was a way to make their lives fit together. Maybe Seb's new world didn't have to be in conflict with his old world.

Maybe. Squeezing into the fur-covered back seat of Brock's station wagon, 'maybe' seemed like a more hopeful word than it had in a long time.

THE CROWD WAS BIGGER THAN Trey expected, and there were more different kinds of people than he'd thought there would be. Lots of people who clearly weren't from the neighborhood, and that worried him more than he wanted to admit. He wasn't *scared* of them—nothing that stupid. It was just weird, the way they stared at his battered face, but weird wasn't a big deal. Was it?

"You're a celebrity," Tristan said from beside him.

"What?"

"They recognize you from the interview." Tristan looked—proud? Was that possible? Oh, proud of Simon—he'd been the one who'd made the interview happen.

"Yeah, I guess. It was a good idea to do that."

"And you did it well." Tristan smiled at him, then went back to scanning the crowd, seeming almost as nervous as Trey was. "You got way more people here than we expected."

"Not *me*."

"Yeah, you. I mean, you and Seb." A sideways look that Trey probably wasn't supposed to notice. "You heard from him yet?"

"What? Today? No. Why would I have?"

Tristan's snort of impatience was much more familiar than his other expressions. "Come on, Trey! You heard him in the interview—in an *interview*, one he knew would be played in front of everybody he knows. You saw how he looked."

"He looked—he just looked like Seb. What are you talking about?"

"He was so apologetic. So, like, genuinely affected by what had happened."

"Yeah—he was working with us and then it turned out he was kind of on the other side. He's not a bad guy—of course he'd be affected."

"Jesus, Trey. He was talking about *you*. Trying to apologize to *you*."

Trey let his eyes go back to scanning the crowd. He wasn't sure what he was searching for, exactly, but he didn't want to be looking at Tristan right then. Didn't want Tristan to be looking at him, really, because feeling like this? Uncertain and confused, strangely hopeful at the same time as horribly vulnerable? Hell, no, there was no need for Tristan to see any of that playing out on Trey's face.

So he kept his focus on the distance, and that's where he saw them. *Him*, but, also, *them*.

Because Seb was with his family. His friends. It didn't matter that Seb had no personal photos on his apartment wall, because Trey didn't need that kind of evidence to know who these people were. They were all just so clean. Not that Trey wasn't clean in a technical sense—he'd done laundry the night before and showered that morning—but that kind of stuff didn't matter, not in the face of cleanness like Seb and his friends had. Like the world had never touched them, never made them crawl through grime. Like they didn't even know what dirt *was*.

Seb turned to the guy next to him and grinned at something he'd said. Trey's chest hurt. Just his ribs; he must have taken a deep breath or something. That was all. Nothing to do with how perfect it was to see Seb so relaxed, so happy.

"You going to go say hi?" Tristan asked.

Trey scowled at him. "No. Why would I?"

"No reason, I guess." Tristan seemed suddenly impatient. "So come with me to find Simon and we'll get this thing started. It's time to march."

Marching. Going for a walk, as if that was going to change anything.

But it was the whole point of the day, so Trey obediently followed Tristan up the small hill to where the rest of the team was clustered under a huge banner.

He stood still while Simon said a few words into the microphone, and while two other community members gave their short speeches. There was some cheering, but that wasn't going to do any more good than going for a walk was going to do.

Nothing was going to do any good. Nothing was going to change. And that just made it more important that Trey stay tough, stay strong, and stay ready. The world was always going to be rough, so he needed to make sure he was on guard and prepared to step in whenever his friends needed his help. That was his job.

Tristan's job was to be kind and keep his friends together; Simon's job was to be smart and organize things; Shane's job *used* to be pretty similar to Trey's, but now he had Noah and Dodger and only needed to look after them. So Trey needed to step up and look out for everyone himself.

And Seb? Seb's job was to—

Trey's attention was caught by the man waving his arms from across the square. Older, wearing too many clothes for the weather, looking generally sloppy and worn—Trey didn't know the guy's name, but he recognized him. He slept at the men's shelter when the weather was bad, in the Jungle most of the rest of the time. He was one of the guys Trey and Becks had spoken to back when this was all starting. And now he was jumping around, trying to get Trey's attention and direct it—

Trey's brain stopped working. At least the part of it that could form words and decide what roles different people played. Instead, he kicked over into pure instinct and emotion.

Fear. He didn't like that first flash, but there it was. He squinted at the three men across the square, the ones the old guy had been pointing out. Trey knew them. He could still hear their voices, swearing at him as he struggled. He could feel them grabbing him, holding him, punching, kicking—

"Get Shane," Trey said. He didn't sound scared, and as soon as he spoke, as soon as he started moving, the fear started to drain away. "Tell him to meet me over there, on the far side of it all."

"What?" Tristan demanded.

The speeches were over now and the crowd was moving, slow but steady, flowing out of the little square and down the carless street. It made it hard to hear much, and hard to move in the opposite direction, the way Trey wanted to.

"The guys," Trey yelled. "The ones who got me. They're here." And there was no good reason for that, not unless they were going to stir up more trouble. Which it was Trey's job to prevent. *"Get Shane!"* Two against three still wasn't great odds, especially not with Trey at half-strength, but it was a hell of a lot better than Trey trying to take them on by himself.

"Wait!" Tristan ordered, but there was no time for that. Trey had already lost sight of the men; if he got closer fast enough he might be able to find them again, but if he gave them more time to blend into the crowd?

Hell, no. They weren't going to get away from him.

"Get Shane," he yelled back over his shoulder. "And anyone else!" But mostly Shane.

He didn't wait to see if Tristan was on the job; of course he would be.

He'd be too late, though; no point pretending otherwise. By the time Tristan found Shane, and then the two of them found Trey—

But Trey didn't need to charge in.

He kept moving, but for once his brain was working at the same time as his body.

He could just find the guys, and watch them. He could wait for a good chance, wait for backup. Hell, he could get super-ambitious and try to make some sort of a *plan*, but that was a bit much.

Still, he could at least wait.

Assuming he ever managed to find the guys, which was seeming less and less likely.

He shouldered his way through the crowd, ignoring the pain from his ribs and the scowls from marchers, working toward the last place he'd seen the intruders. It got easier to move as the main body of protesters moved past, easier to see as—

There. Three men in dark hoodies, their backs toward him as they ambled along with the last of the crowd. Trey fell in behind them, about a half-a-block back. He was playing it cool. He wasn't rushing in. Seb would be proud of—

No, of course Seb wouldn't be too impressed by Trey managing to use one or two brain cells at the same time. But Trey needed to stop thinking about Seb anyway.

The men stopped walking, and Trey slowed down. Then he saw them looking around, scanning the crowd, and forced himself to turn his head away. Would they still recognize him from the side?

They could have if they'd tried a little harder, but of course they weren't looking for him, he realized. They were looking for cops. And they hadn't found any.

They started forward with more purpose, now. If they hadn't already smashed his cell phone he could have called Shane and given him directions, because it was clear where they were heading. The Nguyen's corner store.

They might just need a pack of cigarettes, he told himself. This didn't have to be a big deal. But he'd been around too many guys like these—hell, if he was honest, he'd *been* a guy like these, at least in smaller ways—and he could recognize the controlled excitement in their movements.

There was no more time for waiting. Trey broke into a jog just as the men pulled black bandanas up over their faces.

They were going to smash things up. Make it look like the protest had been violent, get some footage of their bullshit on the news. Make it easy for their corporate masters to spread the story that the protesters were thugs, not citizens.

"Hey!" Trey bellowed. If there were any cameras turned in this direction, they could at least get a shot of someone fighting back against the assholes. Someone getting killed in the process, probably, but that was a chance he'd take. It was his job, after all. "Hey, you! I know you!"

All three turned to face him. The tallest one stepped forward. "Are you fucking kidding? You're back for *more*? You're lucky you're still alive, motherfucker. You want, we can change that."

"Yeah, you're a fucking tough guy when it's three to one."

"It's *still* three to one."

Yeah, it was. Wherever Shane was, he hadn't made it over in time. But, fuck it. Trey wouldn't run.

But then a voice came from off to the side. "It's not three to one," Seb said, sounding as calm and cool as if he was correcting a kid learning basic math.

Trey's whole body froze, then jerked around. "No," he told Seb. "This isn't for you." Of course it wasn't for him. It was too gritty, too real. What was Seb thinking? "It's not safe. Go find Shane."

Seb didn't move, though, and the people behind him—all his golden, happy friends and family—drew closer. Two of them had phones up, filming the scene.

"I've got the police on the line," the older man said. "And there are a lot of witnesses here. Your employers won't want you to continue with your plan now that you've been recognized."

"Fuck you," the tall one spat back.

Yeah, Trey could have predicted that. These guys were pumped up and ready to fight; they weren't going to back down because some old guy in khakis presented an opinion.

"I won't let you mess with that store," Trey said. Simpler, easier for them to understand. Equally pointless, of course, but at least the people filming might catch the words and anyone who watched would understand that this wasn't some sort of gang fight. Protesters were *protecting* the store, not damaging it.

He stepped toward them, and the tall guy moved to meet him, the other two trailing in his wake.

But Seb was coming forward, too. And the others. Jesus, Seb's mom, the fancy doctor, was marching forward like she was ready for a damn brawl.

"It'll be different this time," the older guy, surely Seb's dad, said. "I'm ashamed that you were able to hurt any citizen of this city and get away with it. But if you hurt any of us? Trust me. There will be *consequences*."

But consequences wouldn't do any good if Seb was already hurt. Didn't his dad see that? Why was he letting this happen? What the hell could Trey do to stop it?

He thought about running. If he left, would the others back down? The Nguyens probably had insurance or something for their store. It would be wrong; it would mean Trey hadn't done what he was on the planet to do. But at least Seb wouldn't get hurt.

He'd actually taken a cautious step back when he caught movement out of the corner of his eye. A half-turn of his head was enough to tell him the entire situation had just changed dramatically.

Because Shane was there, big and tough and ready to do what needed to be done. Tristan and Noah beside him, Simon, Micah—and Jake. Jake's face a mask of hatred as he brushed past Shane and stalked toward the men. "You the assholes who like to start fires?" he said, his voice low and menacing.

Because Trey getting beat up wasn't the worst thing that had happened lately, not by a long shot. Jake's brother had died in a fire that someone had started. And these three seemed to be the go-to thugs for whoever was pulling the strings on all this.

The men were surrounded now, and the crowd was edging in closer.

"We need to stay calm," Seb's dad said. "The police are on their way. They'll arrest these men, and they'll face charges. There'll be a full investigation."

"There hasn't been much of an investigation so far," Jake said, his gaze still locked on the three men.

"There will be this time," a new voice said. A young woman, probably a couple years older than Seb, with the same bright eyes and blond hair. She was standing beside him, and her gaze was just as confident and strong as his. "I've already spoken to one of the partners in my law firm. He's very active in municipal affairs and has the mayor's ear. He's going to push on this one." Her expression softened, and Trey could tell she knew who Jake was even before she added, "We can't bring your brother back. But this won't be pushed under the rug. I promise."

Even with the strong words and the promise, Trey honestly wasn't sure which way Jake was going to go. He knew he'd back Jake up either way, though.

As it happened, the decision was made for them. A siren meeped from somewhere nearby and most of the crowd turned to see the police car approaching with lights flashing. Most of the crowd turned. But Trey kept his eyes on the three men, so he saw it when the tall man turned, started to run—and when Jake grabbed him by the shoulder, spun him around, and landed a crushing blow to his jaw.

The other two started to run but Shane was there, and somehow Trey was involved as well, grappling and wrestling more than really fighting, but with broken ribs and a brace on his hand it was more than enough action. After a few seconds, when the cops were closer, he let himself be guided away by a firm, kind grasp, and when he was clear of the scuffle he somehow wasn't surprised to find Seb beside him, his worried eyes locked on Trey's.

"Your ribs," Seb whispered.

"His zygomatic arch," Dr. Tanner said more forcefully. She stepped in front of Trey, at least six inches shorter than him and with absolutely no doubt of her own authority. "Were there any blows to your face? Any pressure?" She held up a finger. "Track my fingertip, please. Then we'll review the state of your hand."

It was all too bewildering, and impossible to resist, especially since Trey didn't truly *want* to resist. He was perfectly happy to have this woman bossing him around, taking care of him; perfectly happy to have Seb standing beside him, looking concerned but not actually scared; happy to see the police taking charge of the assholes, even if that meant justice would come from a court instead of from the hands and feet of their victims.

"Are you okay?" Seb asked quietly when his mother was done asking more demanding questions.

"I'm fine," Trey said. He looked over to where Jake was cradling his wrist, Micah hovering anxiously by his side. "I bet Jake busted his hand, though."

"I'll need X-rays to be sure of that," Dr. Tanner said. She turned to her son and smiled. "Thank you for arranging this. You knew I'm not comfortable in big crowds or with social issues, so you found a way to get me back to my comfort zone. You're a lovely son."

Trey stared at her. Was she being funny, or mean? Just how much sarcasm was she dealing out?

Based on Seb's return grin, there was nothing to worry about. "Micah can take Jake to the hospital," he said sweetly. "I don't think you need to go with them."

"Oh, I do," she replied. "Once I begin caring for a patient, I like to see things through to the end."

"You haven't actually begun yet," Seb started, but already his mother was on the move.

"I'm Dr. Emma Tanner," she said, smooth and professional as she approached Jake. "We need to immobilize your arm for the trip to the hospital." And Jake let himself be washed into the same river of caring management that Trey had been enjoying.

Which left Trey on the sidelines, of course. With Seb.

"You're missing the protest," Trey said. "We can catch up to them." He felt suddenly awkward, as if he was in the wrong place at the wrong time. And, he forced himself to remember, with the wrong person.

"We'll need to talk to the police." Seb looked over toward the three squad cars that had arrived in the last minute or so. "Give a statement."

Trey knew the right answer: he had nothing to say to the police. They were the enemy.

But the three guys were flat on the ground, cuffed, their bandanas pulled down to expose their faces. Was the enemy of his enemy his friend? "I already talked to them," he tried. "At the hospital. There's nothing new, really."

"Everything that happened today is new. You being able to identify them as the guys who jumped you is new. You need to talk to the police. Absolutely." A pause as if Seb was thinking, was wondering, and then he said, "And I'm in charge."

The words hung there, as if Seb was waiting. As if the whole damn world was waiting.

There was no denying that everything happening right then was real life, and that meant, by the terms of their deal, that Seb was right. He was the one who should be making the decisions. But the deal wasn't real; or maybe it had been, for a few strange and perfect days, but it wasn't anymore. It couldn't be.

"You don't want that kind of responsibility," Trey said. "It's like feeding the birds in the winter. Once you start feeding them, you aren't supposed to stop. They're counting on you now, and if you stop they'll be in trouble."

"I don't want to stop." Seb looked around, clearly aware that there was an audience, even if everyone was doing a fairly good job of pretending to ignore the conversation. "And you're not a bird. You can count on me. If you can trust me again, you can count on me. But it doesn't mean you'd be in trouble without me. It just means—" Another look at the people around them, a grimace, and then, "Fuck. Can you just—can we—for now, can you trust me enough to stay and talk to the police? And then after—after the protest, if we still have time to go to that, or after the police or just whenever, at some point—can we talk? Can we just—if I have to walk away, I'll walk away, but I don't want to *give up.* Not until I know I have to. Can you just give me a bit of your time?"

It would be better to say no. Smarter. And saying no would mean Trey wouldn't have to talk to the police, which would definitely be a plus.

But he'd be damned if he'd let some rich junior suit be tougher than him. If Seb wanted to fight this out to the end, then Trey would have to fight it out, too.

So he gave a grumpy shrug and shifted around so he could lean against the building and glare at the cops. That was his agreement. Seb eased around beside him and they stood shoulder to shoulder, backs to the wall. Trey tried to ignore how right it felt.

Chapter Twenty-two

THE REST OF THE PROTEST went smoothly, at least for the crowd as a whole. Seb, unfortunately, was experiencing jitters of a sort he'd never imagined. Not the fun butterflies of anticipation before a big event. No, not this time. Instead of butterflies he had—ostriches? Something huge and heavy flopping around in his gut every time he brushed against Trey, or looked at him, or thought about him, or even thought about looking at him or brushing against him, or…

It was unpleasant.

At the same time, Seb couldn't seem to stop brushing or looking or thinking, so either his masochism was taking a whole new form, or there was something he liked about the situation.

The police didn't do more than take names and contact information from most of the crowd, but as anticipated they'd been a bit more interested in what Trey had to say, and of course Seb had stayed with him while he gave his preliminary statement in the back room of the Nguyen's store. He was pleased and proud that the rest of his crew, his friends and family, made sure he was okay and then went on to finish the march. A good reminder that they weren't just there to support him; they actually believed in the cause.

"Who's the guy with the yellow shirt?" Trey asked when the police were off conferring for a few minutes.

Seb had to think it through. "Brock? Was Brock wearing yellow? My age, dark hair—"

"You guys are pretty tight." Not quite an accusation, but a bit of extra edge to it. It probably wasn't a good sign that the possibility of jealousy made Seb want to do a celebratory dance.

"He's my cousin. My oldest friend. Yeah, we're tight." Seb watched Trey chew through that, then added, "Even if the cousin thing wasn't gross, he's totally straight."

Trey shrugged as if that was the last piece of information he could ever be interested in, but his shoulders lowered by at least an inch. Yeah, he'd been jealous, and yeah, knowing that made Seb far happier than it should have.

By the time the police were done with them the protest was over. Apparently there'd been news crews and interviews and everything else that had been hoped for, and Seb was happy about all that; he really was. But as soon as the police were done with them he could see Trey getting restless, looking for his escape, and it was hard to be happy about something in the abstract when something so concrete and so important looked like it was trying to get away.

"You don't have to talk to me," he said when they were back out on the sidewalk. "I mean, if you're done with it—if you're done with me—you can just walk away. This doesn't have to be a big scene if you don't want one."

"I absolutely don't want a big scene." Trey looked down the street in the direction of Tristan's apartment, then back at Seb. "What do you want to talk about?"

Jesus. What *did* he want to talk about? How could he put it into words? "I didn't know I owned shares in the real estate company."

"Yeah, I know. Don't worry about it."

"But—you left after you found out. So obviously it's an issue, right? Everything was—I mean, it sucked that you were all beat up. But other than that? I—I liked it. Having you at my place... being friends, or whatever we were being. Friends with maybe potential for more, once you're feeling better. I liked that; I—if there's any way to go back to that, I want to make it happen." There. That was clear enough, wasn't it?

Clear enough for Trey to shake his head over it, at least. "You don't really want that, though. I mean—not doing it the way I'd want it."

A tiny blaze of hope sprang up to join the flames from Trey being jealous. "So—there's a way you'd want it? What would that be?"

Trey grimaced. Frustrated by not having the right words? Seb could absolutely sympathize. "I don't want to be—I mean, I think it's crazy that you're all hung up on liking rough sex. You know I think that. But that's your business, not mine. But I don't want to be your dirty little secret, man." He straightened his shoulders and spoke as if the words were heavy. "I'm not dirty. Being with me— I'm not as clean as you guys, you and your family. I get that. But—I'm not—"

"Shit, no! I'm so sorry, I never—no. I never meant it like that. I never—" Seb caught himself. He'd been about to say he'd never *thought* of Trey that way, but would it be completely true? He wasn't sure, and he didn't have time to puzzle through it all right then. "I don't think of you that way, not at all. I don't even think of myself that way, not really. Not anymore. I mean, you were totally right—it's not a big deal. I don't have to be exactly the same as everyone else and fit *completely* into their expectations in order for them to still love me. My family barely blinked when I told them I was gay, and none of my friends care, either. I have no plans to tell them anything more intimate, but—I don't need to be ashamed of it, either. I get that. And I wouldn't be ashamed of being with you."

Trey snorted. "Bullshit. I mean, it's great that you're okay with your tiny, barely-even-a-thing little kink. That's good. But *me*? I'm saying—I mean, maybe, someday, when things have cooled down a bit, maybe you could give me a call and I'd come over and we could fuck or whatever, the way you do with the other assholes—and I *wouldn't* let it get out of hand, wouldn't let you get hurt—but that's not the same as me staying at your apartment. I mean, you don't want us to *live together*, Seb. That's not what you want."

"No, don't tell me what I don't want. Don't even try it. If *you* don't want something, fine, that's what we can talk about. But what I want?" Shit. He had to do it. He'd tried honesty in the interview and Trey might have seen it and maybe that was why they were having this conversation right now, but it hadn't been enough. He had to go even further. "I like you. I mean, I *care about* you. Like—it's fast, obviously, but, yeah, I want us to live together. In the same room, even, because I really like the idea of going to sleep next to you and waking up together the next morning, and it's totally freaking me out that I want that because I've never even been *close* to wanting it before, and now it seems like it might not matter what I want because it's not what you want. And like I said, if it's not what you want then I'll just have to deal with that. But if there's even a chance that you might be into it? Like, if you were willing to give it a damn try? I'd really like that." He took a deep breath. "And if there's stuff that's getting in the way of you wanting it—like, if you could see how it might be good, but there are certain aspects you're worrying about—then do me the fucking favor of letting me know what they are so I can at least try to deal with them."

"You need me to spell it out? Fuck, Seb, look at yourself. Then look at me. Then look at your family and your friends and my friends and our totally different worlds and different lives. You're—you're a fucking prince of the city, and I'm just some bum who can't even keep himself from getting beat up or find himself a place to sleep without mooching off friends. You're a winner and I'm a loser, and you don't want—fuck. I. *I* don't want to drag you down."

"You've got friends who love you. You're a good person who looks out for other people and tries to take care of them. I don't look at you and see a loser."

"Everyone else will."

"I don't think so, but if they do? Fuck them."

"Yeah, sure. You're just going to walk away from everyone else, everyone who cares about you."

"No. Have you not been listening? They love me. I can be different and they'll still love me. They'll like you or they won't like you, and if they don't like you we'll probably end up fighting about it—them and me, not you and me—and that'll still be okay. Shit, Trey, would your friends dump you if you started dating someone different from them?"

"Different from them? You mean like you?"

"Okay, yeah, like me. They've been putting up with me because I'm trying to be useful, but they don't really like me."

"Yeah they do. You're not the same as us, but they're cool with that."

"And your friends are just way more liberal and accepting and generous than my friends? That's what you think?"

"No, it's not—" Trey rubbed his jaw, winced when his hand brushed over his broken cheek, then shook his head. "Your guys would be *right* to think I'm not good enough for you. My guys would wonder what the hell you were thinking, and they'd be pissed if they thought you were going to mess with me, but they wouldn't think I was slumming, or lowering myself or—"

"Hey." It came out sharp enough to cut Trey short. "Whatever comes of this—whatever you decide, because I've already made it pretty clear what I want—I consider you a friend. And I don't let people talk shit about my friends, so watch what you're saying."

Trey made a little sound that might have been a laugh, and he looked down, and then looked back up with a beautiful, shy expression. "You're serious about this? You really think—" He shook his head, hard. "No. You're just worked up. Adrenaline or something. But think about all the shit you've got that I don't have. No family, no car, no education, no future—"

"Jesus Christ, Trey, what was today about? What was *all of this* about? We've been fighting against this bullshit mentality, and now you're the one spouting it? Some assholes thought you or your friends weren't worth anything so they killed them and beat them up, and you fought back. All of you. You said, 'no, fuck you, we *are* worth something. We *do* matter.' And people heard you, Trey! This protest? People are paying attention to it, and they're believing what you told them. So you need to start believing it yourself. You've got a future if you just have the balls to want one. And for the rest of it?" Seb shook his head. "For the rest? The money stuff? The next time I talk about the Power Imbalance you'd better not fucking laugh at me, asshole! It's a real thing, or at least it could be, if we aren't careful. But we *can* be careful. *I* can be careful and make sure I don't assume stuff I shouldn't, and you can be careful to remind me when I'm missing something, and it can work. I know it can."

Trey paused long enough to make it clear he was running through all his arguments and seeing if any of them still worked. Finally he said, "So—if we were going to do this—if we were going to try—what would that look like?"

Seb swallowed hard and made sure he was ready to sound calm before saying, "You could come stay at my place. On any terms you want. You don't like Tristan's couch and you know you like my guest bed—don't even pretend it's not comfy—so you could just stay in there if you wanted to take it slow. I think I'm mostly out of soup but I can get some more. We could just go back to the way it was, and see—you know. See where it goes. Or we could skip it along a few steps. I'm not sure how much you're up to, with the ribs and all, but I'd be up for pretty much anything, really, if you wanted."

Another long pause and then, "Is there curried chicken soup left? I liked the curried chicken."

Seb was pretty sure he was going to explode if he didn't find a release for the happiness burbling up inside his chest, but he didn't want to go too big too fast and scare Trey away. "I'm not sure," he managed. "You want to come over and we'll see?"

"We should go to Tristan's. There might be stuff going on, stuff we should know about. But—after. Maybe later, I could—we could—I mean, it's really good soup."

Not quite the declaration of devotion Seb might have been hoping for, but it was enough. It was a start. "Yeah. Okay. We can go to Tristan's and then go to my place and see if there's any soup."

He half-turned, but Trey grabbed his hand, then his shoulder, and tugged him around. Edged him sideways, backed him against the brick wall of the store, caught Seb's hair in one big, strong hand, and tugged. Manhandled and arranged and then held in place, and Seb's breath caught at the perfection of it.

"I'm not up for anything too ambitious," Trey growled. He stepped closer, pushed his thigh between Seb's legs like it belonged there, and brought their faces close, his hand still tight and controlling in Seb's hair. "But we can do better than soup."

Seb swallowed hard and then Trey's lips were on his. Not a rough kiss, nothing that would cause trouble for Trey's cheek. But Trey was in charge, taking what he wanted, and Seb was more than ready to give it to him.

Of course, they were on a public street, and Trey at least seemed to have his brain working well enough to remember that. He pulled his lips away before things got too heated but kept his grip on Seb's hair a little bit longer. "Just so we're clear—I have no hesitations at all about the sex part. I'm totally down for that. It's all the rest of it that I'm not sure about."

"That's cool," Seb said. "I'm the one in charge of all the rest of it, right?" He grinned suddenly, all his relief and excitement coming out in a burst of cockiness. "You fuck me right, and I'll make everything else in your life a damn paradise."

Trey smiled back at him and his grip on Seb's hair turned into something closer to a caress. "Like I said, I'm not sure how much I can manage right away. But I don't have to be at full strength to show you who's boss, do I?"

"No, sir," Seb said, and the word felt like an endearment, not a performance.

Judging from the way Trey licked his lips, he didn't object. "Or we could just *call* Tristan," he suggested. "No point in going all the way over there if there's nothing going on."

Tristan's apartment was only a few blocks away, but Seb nodded anyway. "Okay. I'll call him. And I'll call us a cab, 'cause I drove over here with Brock and I don't know where the hell he's gotten to, and tomorrow I'm going to dig up an old cell phone from somewhere and you'll damn well carry it. Because that's life, and I'm in charge of life."

"Until I say you're not."

"Yeah. Just like me and sex."

"Okay," Trey agreed. "Until either one of says differently."

It wasn't exactly death-do-you-part, but that was okay. It was better than okay, really. Seb had no idea where this thing was going to go. But he was pretty damn interested in finding out.

Epilogue

Part One

"THIS ISN'T A GOOD IDEA." Trey had said the same thing several times over the last few days, and the words didn't seem to be getting any less true.

But Seb didn't seem to be getting any more concerned about them. "It's a good *idea*. It might not work out, and if it doesn't, that'll suck. But it won't be the *idea*'s fault."

Trey picked nervously at the seam of his jeans. Seb had suggested something dressier, something more fitting to the occasion, but Trey didn't *have* anything dressier and he wasn't going to buy new clothes—or worse, let Seb buy him new clothes—when he was pretty sure jeans were the best bet anyway.

They weren't meeting at Seb's fancy apartment because Trey didn't want it to seem like he was pretending to be someone he wasn't, and the same went for clothes.

"Is that them?" Seb asked, and Trey jerked his head toward the diner door.

Then he turned to Seb. "Those women are, like, fifty. My sisters are thirteen and fifteen." Crazy to think they'd gotten even that old, but they sure as hell weren't middle-aged.

"One of them could have been your mom. Maybe she changed her mind about coming."

"Stop living in a fairy tale." Because *Seb's* mom was fine with meeting her son's boyfriend, even fine with inviting him to her home and teaching him to make soup, but Trey's mom? He was just glad she was letting the girls come see him.

At least, he hoped she was. He checked his watch. Ten minutes late. That wasn't much.

But the diner was just down the street from the girls' house. There wasn't much potential for things to go wrong on the walk. But what if things had gone wrong before that? Trey's mom hadn't been thrilled about the meeting, but she'd gone along with it. Her boyfriend, though? Had they told him? Had he done something to—

"Wow," Seb said, and Trey turned back to the doorway. "They look like you, but they're really pretty. How did they manage that?"

But Trey was barely listening. He was on his feet, practically stumbling forward, and his sisters were rushing toward him and then they were all wrapped up in a big ball of hugging and possibly a little blubbering.

"You got so big," Trey managed when they all came up for a little air.

"*We* did?" Sefi retorted. God, even her voice was new, a grown woman's voice coming from her grown woman's face.

Talia unwrapped herself from around him long enough to say, "You're so big I can barely hug you," before she went back to proving how well she could manage despite his size.

Trey looked over their heads and found Seb smiling at them. Actually, most of the restaurant seemed to be watching and smiling, but Trey didn't care about them. Only about Seb.

"Thank you," he mouthed. This had all been Seb's brilliant idea, and he'd been just the right amount of pushy in convincing Trey to give it a try.

"Love you," Seb mouthed back.

Yeah, he did. It had taken a while to get used to the idea—a while to get used to a lot of ideas, from Trey moving back to the apartment, then into Seb's bed, then spending time with his family and his friends—but the idea that Seb could love *him*, could say it and mean it—that had been the biggest one.

But Seb had proved it with patience and humor and respect, and he'd given Trey the space to accept the words and return them in his own time. And that had been enough to make—no, to *let* Trey believe.

"Come here," he said now, not sure if he was speaking to his sisters or to Seb. He just knew he wanted them all in the same space, so he urged the girls forward to meet Seb as he came toward them. "Guys, this is my boyfriend, Seb. And these are my sisters, Sefi and Talia."

"Sefina," Sefi corrected. Right, she was all grown up now.

But Talia made a rude noise. "She's still Sefi—nobody calls her Sefina."

"But Sefina is what you prefer?" Seb asked like some kind of gentleman from a movie.

"Yeah, it is," she said with a pointed glare at her sister.

"Sefina. I'm so happy to meet you." And just like that, Seb had himself a fan. He turned to Talia. "I have an older sister, too. It's the baby's job to keep the older ones from getting away with too much, right?"

"It's not easy," Talia agreed, and she beamed.

So, both of the Fiso girls were well on their way to being almost as crazy about Seb as Trey was. And that was just as it should be.

Everything was just as it should be.

*****

Part Two

"IT'S A PLEA BARGAIN," the detective explained, as if he had to. As if Jake had never watched TV and didn't know what was going on. At least the detective had the courage to come over and tell Jake to his face. "We couldn't get enough evidence to convict the others, not without cooperation from these three. So—lesser charges for them, at least for the fires. Manslaughter instead of murder, but they'll still do time. And aggravated assault for the attack on Mr. Fiso, plus a few other charges—and they all have criminal records. They'll be in jail for a good stretch, no question."

"And with their testimony—you'll be able to get the others? The guys behind it all?" Micah was next to Jake on the sofa of their small apartment, his hand resting protectively on Jake's thigh.

The detective nodded slowly. "We have a strong case. The investigation is ongoing—we know the core group who were behind it, and we're just trying to figure out how far the involvement might have spread. But for the two men behind it all? We anticipate a conviction, and jail time."

"Just jail time," Jake said. "I mean—you're going to charge them with murder, right? And conspiracy and all the rest of it? They should get locked up with the key thrown away!"

"I agree. But—" The detective stretched his hands out as if surrendering to powers beyond his control. "They've got some excellent lawyers, and they did a reasonably good job of insulating themselves from the more serious crimes committed in their interests. I'd love to tell you they're going to be gone forever, but realistically—I expect we'll see plea bargains there, too. If the case isn't an absolute slam dunk the prosecutor will likely try to deal with them as well. Make sure they get at least *some* jail time."

Jake stared at him. After all the pain, all the fighting, it had come down to this? Some lifelong criminals would get a little more jail time and some rich men would get a slap on the wrist? "My brother is *dead*," he choked out.

The detective nodded his understanding but didn't have much more to say.

"So we'll go see Simon," Micah said after the detective left. "He says there are more options—we'll go hear them."

"Or just give up." The words tasted bitter in Jake's mouth, but he felt like they needed to be said. "Stop fighting and just move on."

"We *are* moving on," Micah responded. "You and me—we're not, like, wallowing in the past, are we? Your business is doing great, you and me are doing great—it's not like we're consumed by the need for revenge, is it? I mean—yeah. If you want to quit, we can quit. But if it's up to me? Hell, no. I think we've got lots of fight left."

"Does it make it harder for you?" Jake should have asked this earlier, in a calmer situation. But better late than never, hopefully. "I mean, you're doing so well—working the program, at least your version of it, and starting to help other people and everything. Would it be easier for you if we had one less thing to worry about? If we just shut the door on all that history?"

"Easier?" Micah grinned, the teasing, sexy smile that drove Jake crazy. "Since when are we about what's *easier*? Come on, man. You and me, we don't look for things that are *easy*, do we? We look for things that are good. So if letting go of Austin is what's good for you, then that's what we'll do. But if it's good to keep on fighting for justice? Then *that's* what we'll do. Your call."

"Damn." Jake tugged on Micah's arm pulling him closer, dragging both of their bodies out on the couch until they were closer to horizontal. "You're like my personal motivational speaker." A kiss, more than a peck but not too serious. Yet. "My counsellor, my therapist."

"I prefer 'growth guru'," Micah said, and the kiss this time was deeper. He pulled away long enough to say, "It works especially well because you're in landscaping. You get it? Growth?"

"Wow. That's profound." He dragged his hands across Micah's ribs, down his back, and got a good grip on his ass, pulling their bodies together at all the right spots. "When was Simon expecting us over there? Have we got time?"

"You're sure you want to go? Don't let me pressure you into it."

"I want to go. But not quite yet...."

Micah rocked his pelvis into Jake's. "We've got time," he said. "We've got the whole rest of our lives."

*****

Part Three

EVEN AFTER MONTHS OF BEING with Tristan, months of working with his friends and his community, Simon still felt like he was perpetually auditioning for his place in the group. Constantly having to prove himself.

The frustrating part was how important it was that he do so. He shouldn't care about these people. Tristan was one thing—he was worth any sacrifice to Simon's dignity or self-regard. But the rest of them? Why the hell did he care so much?

"It's a two-pronged approach," he said now, presenting his ideas to Jake with as much care as any proposal he'd ever made to his uncle. "But they're obviously interconnected, and should be effective in different ways. The civil lawsuit is a way to hit them in the pocketbook, obviously. The PR campaign will have to be more subtle—we want to be sure we don't run into issues of defamation. But I truly believe that most people in the world are good people, and the more they learn about this case, the more appalled they'll be. We've seen this already in the support for the community group and the freeze on development permits in the neighborhood. We've essentially won the fight in terms of protecting our neighbors. Now we're looking for justice. So the lawsuit will affect them financially, while a subtle PR campaign, based *mostly* around publicizing the evidence presented in the lawsuit, will hurt them in other ways. And, just as significantly, it will send a clear message."

Jake frowned, then nodded. "Like a social shaming," he said.

"It's been used too often to hurt innocent people," Tristan said, "but it's an excellent way to reinforce community values. Gay people, non-Christians—anyone who didn't fit in—shaming was used as a weapon against them too damn often. It doesn't just punish them, it reinforces the status quo with everyone else, makes it clear what behaviour is or isn't acceptable."

"So we'd be using a bad tool for a good purpose," Micah said thoughtfully.

"The only bad tool is an ineffective tool," Simon said. He should probably be keeping his mouth shut, but after all the months of playing it safe, it might be time for him to assert himself a little. "Tools are neither moral nor immoral—they're just tools. This tool has been used in the past for ugly things, but that's because of the ugliness in the people using the tool, not the tool itself."

"And it's effective," Micah mused. He turned to Jake. "This makes sense to me. Shame them, not just for justice, but for—I don't know, for reinforcing the right values. These guys fucked up. They thought money was more important than human beings. The shaming will make it clear that they were wrong."

"And the lawsuit will show that even if some people don't *care* about morality, it's still financially unwise to be callous with human lives." Simon waited for a response, and was gratified by Jake's slow nod.

"I don't actually want any money from them. I mean, I don't want blood money, don't want to profit from my brother's death."

"You could apply it to good causes," Simon said. "I mean, depending on the amount you receive, I'd definitely recommend keeping at least some of it, just in case you or yours have a rainy day. But if it's a large settlement? Which I absolutely think it could be. I've got some ideas for that."

"You've always got ideas," Micah said. "One of my favorite things about you."

Surprising and simultaneously not surprising at all, how hard that plain statement hit Simon. Micah had not one but *multiple* favorite things about Simon. And at least one of them was based on who Simon actually was, as himself, not just as an adjunct to Tristan.

Micah and Jake moved on with the conversation, but Simon took a moment to collect himself, and he felt a familiar hand find his and squeeze. He looked over to see Tristan smiling at him. Because Tristan knew how Simon had been feeling. Of course he did; he was Tristan. And he knew how much Micah's casual words had meant. Again, of course he did.

"It'll be expensive, though, won't it?" Jake's words cut into the peaceful moment. "A lawsuit like this? I mean, I have *some* money, but not that much."

"I have some too," Simon said. "And I have it because you— you and Tristan—gave it to me. You could have kept the gold for yourselves, but you didn't, and—actually, this ties in with my other ideas. But those ideas are for the whole team. We've invited them over for dinner—is it okay if we hold off for a while and talk about it when they're here?"

"Dinner? That we don't have to make ourselves?" Micah leaned back and laced his fingers behind his head. "Sounds perfect."

Simon took the opportunity to go put the chicken in the oven. He was bent over, making sure the roasting pan was far enough in, when he felt gentle pressure along his legs. He straightened, and Tristan's arms wrapped around his waist from behind. "I'm glad you're here," Tristan whispered into his shoulder. "For me, but for everybody else, too. You're good for us. To us. You're good." He pressed a gentle kiss to Simon's neck. "Are we good for you?"

Simon turned a little too quickly for proper balance. "Of course," he said, hoping the fullness of meaning came through in his voice. "You—you especially, but the others too—you're very good for me. You know that."

"I suspected," Tristan confirmed. He looked pleased with himself. No, not with himself, with everybody. Everything. He just looked *pleased*, and it made something in Simon's chest relax to see it. "But it's nice to hear a reminder now and then."

"Whenever you need it," Simon promised.

"And whenever you need it, too." Tristan slid his hands down to find Simon's, interlaced their fingers, and tugged. "Now come have a drink with our friends."

Simon let himself be guided back out to the living room and sat down with Simon's friends. *Their* friends. Their life, together, with all its joys and challenges. He couldn't think of a single part he'd want to change.

*****

Part Four

DODGER HAD NO IDEA WHY humans had to walk so slowly; their noses were up way too high for them to be tracking any interesting scents, so why the hell did it take them so long to get anywhere? He tugged at his leash—another stupid human thing he couldn't really understand—and tried to drag Shane forward.

"No pulling," Shane said, and he reached one of his big paws down, caught Dodger around his belly, and lifted him back to stand next to Shane's legs. Usually it was excellent having a big human to climb on and snuggle with and be protected by, but sometimes it was kind of annoying. Dodger was a big dog now, after all, and Shane shouldn't be able to just pick him up like he was still a little pup!

"He knows where we're going," Noah said. "They spoil him rotten, you know."

"Yeah, but so do I, when you're not looking."

The humans jostled their shoulders, playful and loving, and Dodger wished they were all at the same level so he could join in. Oh well, he'd save his affection for later, when they were all snuggled up on Tristan's couch.

Because, yeah, damn right he knew where they were going. It was a pretty safe bet, since they spent so much time at Tristan's den, and once they turned onto the street it was all confirmed. Familiar smells, familiar sounds, even that weird-ass dog across the street who always barked and growled like he thought he was a tough guy, like Dodger couldn't chew him up and spit him out without even needing any backup from Shane and Noah. Yeah, that dog was stupid to even think about messing with Dodger!

They turned up the walkway, went into the hallway with *so many* interesting layers of smell, then jogged up the stairs. Dodger danced in anticipation as Noah knocked and then pushed the door open, then raced inside as soon as Shane had the stupid leash off.

They were all here! All of them! All the boys, and Becky and Amanda, and the magic doctor who'd fixed him that time he got sick, and her mate—everybody! His favorite people in the whole world, his pack—even the cat, snooty and superior all the time, was part of the gang.

"Whoa, settle down, buddy," Tristan said, and he crouched down so Dodger could give kisses. Damn, Tristan smelled even better than usual—dinner was going to be great!

Visits with everyone took some time, and then there had to be a second round in case anyone had some snacks or petting they'd been saving up for later, and by the time Dodger jumped up onto the couch and wedged himself between Noah and Shane's legs, he was pretty tired. He dozed a little, listening to the humans talk.

"We want to keep working as a team," Simon was saying. Dodger didn't really know what that was about, but he was pretty sure 'team' meant 'pack', so he absolutely agreed it was important that they all stay together that way. "We'll be low on cash to start with, obviously—well, probably low on cash forever. If Jake wants to go ahead with the civil suit—"

"I do," Jake said, and there was something in his voice that made Dodger lift his head and look around. He wasn't sure where the enemy was, but he could tell Jake was planning to teach them a lesson—and obviously he'd want Dodger's help with that.

"Then we'll need to have some money to support our efforts there. We can likely get a lawyer to work on contingency, but there are always extra costs, and Jake at least will be pretty busy with the case at times, so he'll need to keep his savings in case his income dips from doing less work. So—I've still got most of the money from my aunt. If we need it all for the case, we'll use it for that. But otherwise, I'd like to use it for a new organization. And I'd also like to do some fundraising for that organization, piggybacking on the good press we've gotten for the neighborhood protection movement."

That was a lot of big words and Dodger didn't know what most of them meant, but Shane was the next person to speak, so Dodger listened out of loyalty, even if he wasn't getting a lot of the content. "What's the organization *for*?"

"We're not sure about that," Tristan said, and he gave a little laugh that made Dodger's tail wag in appreciation. Laughing was good. Dodger liked it when his people laughed. "But we feel like we have a really good energy going, and we don't want it to fade away just because the neighborhood thing is shifting into a different sphere. I mean, obviously we'd still want to support the animal shelter, and the connections we're making to pet owners that way. And maybe that's enough. But we thought—I mean, I was saying I was going to miss working with you all, and Simon said maybe I didn't have to, and we got about that far and then thought we should come talk to you before we went any further."

Blah, blah, blah. Dodger nudged Shane's hand and he obligingly responded with some ear ruffles, but clearly his attention was mostly on the conversation. Stupid humans, with all their words.

"Really," Tristan said, "It's about something bigger. It's—" He looked over at Simon, clearly hoping for support, then continued. "It's timeless. It's part of something larger. We can look at Foucault, Marx, Machiavelli—it's always about power, and who gets to use their power in which ways. There are always going to be people who try to push other people around. They get some money, some power, and they think it makes them special. There will always be those people, but there'll always be *us*, too. Always be the people who stand up to them and tell them to back off."

Dodger knew all about standing up for himself. And for his pack, obviously. Yeah, that was important. Nobody got to push Dodger or his friends around.

"The protest wasn't designed to flush out the thugs," Simon said. "That was a great side-effect—the assholes behind all this got stubborn and tried to make things worse for us, but instead they flushed themselves out of hiding. It was a gift, but the protest was truly about pushing back. Making sure people don't get pushed around just because they don't have a lot of money or power. And whatever we kept doing? It could be along the same lines. We could find ways to keep fighting for people who need someone to stand up for them."

"I think it's a great idea," Seb said. He was the newest member of the pack, but he clearly made Trey happy, and Dodger liked Trey much more when he was happy. There'd been a few times in the past when Dodger'd been pretty sure Trey and Shane were going to get into a fight, and damn, Trey sure would have been sorry if *that* had happened. Shane on his own would have been tough to beat, but Shane *plus* Dodger? Totally invincible, and Trey should have known it. But since Seb came around, Trey didn't seem nearly as interested in fighting. So Dodger liked Seb. Who was still talking, unfortunately. "I agree about the goodwill we could take advantage of. And my family's been talking about ways to get more involved in community projects—I know we could count on them for financial support, but if you're interested, I think they'd be willing to contribute time as well."

Dodger didn't know what that was about, but the humans all seemed pretty excited about the whole conversation, so that was nice for them. For him? He sniffed the air, then squirmed until he was lying on his back, feet up in the air.

He was warm and dry, and there was chicken cooking only a few steps away. He had Shane, and Noah, and the rest of his pack. Everything was perfect, and he dozed off knowing that he and everyone he loved was safe and happy.

Other Books by Kate Sherwood

(all m/m – for m/f see Cate Cameron at

www.catecameronauthor.com)

Feral – first book in the *Shelter* series – NA contemporary drama

Lap Dog – second book in the *Shelter* series

Twice Shy – third book in the *Shelter* series

Sacrati – fantasy/alt history

In Too Deep – NA contemporary drama

Chasing the Dragon – angst and adventure!

Mark of Cain – contemporary drama

The Fall, Riding Tall – two book contemporary drama

The Shift – contemporary fantasy novella – monster hunters!

Room to Grow – contemporary drama novella

The Pawn, The Knight – two book futuristic drama with plenty of
angst

Poor Little Rich Boy – contemporary drama

More than Chemistry – light contemporary novella

Beneath the Surface – contemporary drama

Dark Horse, Out of the Darkness, Of Dark and Bright – three book
contemporary drama with extras

Shying Away – NA drama

Lost Treasure – contemporary drama

About the Author

Kate Sherwood started writing about the same time she got back on a horse after almost twenty years away from riding. She'd like to think she was too young for it to be a midlife crisis, but apparently she was ready for some changes!

Kate grew up near Toronto, Ontario (Canada) and went to school in Montreal, then Vancouver. But for the last decade or so she's been a country girl. Sure, she misses some of the conveniences of the city, but living close to nature makes up for those lacks. She's living in Ontario's "cottage country"–other people save up their time and come to spend their vacations in her neighborhood, but she gets to live there all year round!

Since her first book was published in 2010, she's kept herself busy with novels, novellas, and short stories in almost all the sub-genres of m/m romance. Contemporary, suspense, scifi or fantasy–the settings are just the backdrop for her characters to answer the important questions. How much can they share, and what do they need to keep? Can they bring themselves to trust someone, after being disappointed so many times? Are they brave enough to take a chance on love?

Kate's books balance drama with humor, angst with optimism. They feature strong, damaged men who fight themselves harder than they fight anyone else. And, wherever possible, there are animals: horses, dogs, cats ferrets, squirrels… sometimes it's easier to bond with a non-human, and most of Kate's men need all the help they can get.

After five years of writing, Kate is still learning, still stretching herself, and still enjoying what she does. She's looking forward to sharing a lot more stories in the future.

Find out more about Kate Sherwood and her books at her website: www.katesherwoodbooks.com

Follow Kate Sherwood on Facebook, too.